SIX GEESE A LAYING

Twelve Days of Christmas

Emily E K Murdoch

ARE YOU SIGNED UP FOR DRAGONBLADE'S BLOG?

You'll get the latest news and information on exclusive giveaways, exclusive excerpts, coming releases, sales, free books, cover reveals and more.

Check out our complete list of authors, too!

No spam, no junk. That's a promise!

Sign Up Here

www.dragonbladepublishing.com

Dearest Reader;

Thank you for your support of a small press. At Dragonblade Publishing, we strive to bring you the highest quality Historical Romance from some of the best authors in the business. Without your support, there is no 'us', so we sincerely hope you adore these stories and find some new favorite authors along the way.

Happy Reading!

CEO, Dragonblade Publishing

Additional Dragonblade books by Author Emily E K Murdoch

Twelve Days of Christmas
Twelve Drummers Drumming
Eleven Pipers Piping
Ten Lords a Leaping
Nine Ladies Dancing
Eight Maids a Milking
Seven Swans a Swimming
Six Geese a Laying
Five Gold Rings
Four Calling Birds

The De Petras Saga
The Misplaced Husband (Book 1)
The Impoverished Dowry (Book 2)
The Contrary Debutante (Book 3)
The Determined Mistress (Book 4)
The Convenient Engagement (Book 5)

The Governess Bureau Series
A Governess of Great Talents (Book 1)
A Governess of Discretion (Book 2)
A Governess of Many Languages (Book 3)
A Governess of Prodigious Skill (Book 4)
A Governess of Unusual Experience (Book 5)
A Governess of Wise Years (Book 6)
A Governess of No Fear (Novella)

Never The Bride Series
Always the Bridesmaid (Book 1)
Always the Chaperone (Book 2)
Always the Courtesan (Book 3)

Always the Best Friend (Book 4)
Always the Wallflower (Book 5)
Always the Bluestocking (Book 6)
Always the Rival (Book 7)
Always the Matchmaker (Book 8)
Always the Widow (Book 9)
Always the Rebel (Book 10)
Always the Mistress (Book 11)
Always the Second Choice (Book 12)
Always the Mistletoe (Novella)
Always the Reverend (Novella)

The Lyon's Den Series
Always the Lyon Tamer

Pirates of Britannia Series
Always the High Seas

De Wolfe Pack: The Series
Whirlwind with a Wolfe

Selina and Arthur and Dorothea
Caroline
Arabella
Sophia
Esther
Lucy
Jemima
London
Rupert and Frances
Joy
Harmony
William and Leonora
Olivia
Katarina
Isabella
Maria
Bath
Chalcroft
Fitzroy

CHAPTER ONE

"CAREFUL, CAREFUL—OH, OVER WE go!"

Laughter rang out in the large drawing room at Chalcroft as Maria rushed forward, flushing, to help up the little toddler from where he had fallen. Panic rose in her heart, and her lungs tightened. It had been her fault—she was the one who was supposed to be looking after him. That was the task her sister had unceremoniously given her, at least, the moment she had arrived.

But baby Tommy giggled up from the floor, examining the ceiling and his aunt's face with equal equanimity. Pudgy hands reached out to grasp her face, entirely missing of course.

"He is fine," Maria said under her breath, mostly to herself, but also so the child's mother could be reassured. "Completely fine."

"Of course he is fine!" snorted her sister Olivia from the arm-chair where she was seated by the fire, heavy bags under her eyes and a newborn in her arms. "Children bounce, Maria, honestly, do not concern yourself."

If Maria had been a different sort of person, she would have frowned, perhaps said that Olivia should be watching her own children if she was so blasé about it all, and that Maria was tired of rushing across the room, skirts flying, to pick up little Tommy.

But she did not. Maria was not the sort of person to speak up against anyone, let alone her oldest sister who had married two years ago—two years ago this very Christmas, in fact.

"Do not concern yourself," said Kitty, the second of the Chalcroft Fitzroy sisters. "He will do quite well to learn how to pick himself up. After all, what does it matter if he falls into the fire or trips down the stairs?"

A wry smile crept across her face as she sat on the sofa with her husband, Isaac, and Maria felt her shoulders relax.

Kitty, or Katarina to anyone who did not wish to die a painful death, was just as beautiful as Olivia but with far more an acerbic wit than the softer spoken, rather prim Olivia.

Maria's shoulders started to loosen as she righted the small boy, and his mother started to object.

"Fall into the fire—Kitty, you cannot be serious!"

The gentle argument flowed over Maria's head. She never got involved if she could help it, leaving the two of them and Isabella, the fourth of the sisters, to their debates.

Her own nature was softer. Quieter. Certainly more afraid of attention than them.

"Peace," said their father, William Fitzroy, as he stepped forward to pick up his grandson. "Little Thomas is safe and well, and that is all that matters."

As usual, the sisters calmed down, and the normal chatter of the season began: holly and ivy for the Christmas wreaths must be collected, the Christmas pudding had been left for too long, or not enough, and just why did Reverend Wells consider now the best time to let the vicarage cottage? To a stranger, no less!

Maria crept to a chair further from the fire and curled up there, watching, eyes darting to and fro as the conversation continued. If she was careful, she could slink away in a few minutes and leave them to discuss the last details of the Christmas preparations. Any excuse not to be with people. Any excuse to be alone.

"—think letting most of the servants off on their holidays early was a mistake," her Papa was saying, mildly without any accusation, to his wife. "We really needed an additional maid and a few more footmen, my dear."

Leonora Fitzroy bristled, her Italian blood rising to the fore, yet a teasing smile danced across her face. "Well! It is my household, William, and if a woman cannot run her own household than the world has become a strange place indeed! It wouldn't hurt you to open your own front door!"

The family laughed: her parents, her sisters, their husbands. Maria smiled weakly.

It was odd, when most of one's siblings were married, Maria mused. The whole family seemed…different, somehow.

It was not as though the Fitzroy family at large was unaccustomed to weddings. Of her eight cousins, four were married, and now two of her own sisters as well.

But it brought a different dynamic to the family. Outsiders. People she barely knew, though they had been married for a few years now—almost four years, in the case of her cousins.

Maria swallowed. She could not be the only one in the world to find it difficult to speak to new people, could she? Sometimes it was hard enough to speak to her own flesh and blood, her own sisters.

"—is that letter from Esther?" Isabella was saying, wandering around the drawing room as the fire blazed, lifting up cushions in hunt of the thing. "She mentioned a most interesting gentleman she had met—Maria, have you seen it?"

Heat seared Maria's cheeks as though she had been found out in a falsehood—which was nonsense, for she had said not a word. "N-No."

Damn her tongue! Maria's thoughts, far more coherent than her words, raged at her for sounding such a fool.

It was bad enough that she would never attract the attention of a gentleman with her reticent tongue; but not even being able to speak properly to her sisters really was a foolish thing indeed.

"No," she said again, more clearly now, but it did not matter. Isabella had already meandered to the other side of the room, chattering away, as was her custom.

"Yes, a very interesting man! She said that they had gone to the opera together, with Lucy and Kendal—no, I have no idea who Kendal is at all, but wasn't he mentioned when they came this summer?"

"Surely that was old Percy Beaufort," interrupted Kitty, and an entirely new argument began.

Maria smiled weakly, watching Tommy totter about the carpet with his grandfather's close eye on him as the conversation meandered back and forth as to the identity of this strange gentleman.

Another Chalcroft Christmas. The same traditions, the same wreaths, the same company.

She should not complain, not really. Since Kitty and Olivia had married and left Chalcroft for their new homes, the place had been rather quiet indeed. Isabella had still been here of course, but Maria had spent much of the year alone. Quiet. Without being disturbed.

With a sigh, Maria wondered whether she should have done. Alone, in the quiet, in solitude…it was not exactly the best situation in which to find a husband.

A loud knocking echoed in the hall, a knocking that was ignored by the family, save Maria.

Who on earth could it be? Just a week before Christmas, they had no expected callers, no planned visits. The neighbors were away again this Christmas, and there was no one else close for miles.

Yet the identity of the knocker did not appear to interest her family. The conversation had now moved on to whether they would depart Chalcroft for Bath for the rest of the Season.

"You absolutely must come with us," Olivia was saying, eyes bright, leaning forward with excitement. "Balls and concerts, the very best people—"

Kitty made a face. "You and your luxury! Do you not ever just want a simple life, a chance to be…"

The debate was not a new one, and it was not disturbed

when the knocking resumed.

Maria sat up in her chair, looking over at the door to the hall. Someone was at the door—and most importantly, no one had answered. An event most unusual at Chalcroft.

The seat of the Fitzroy family, Chalcroft was a rather large and rambling manor house, and her parents always jested that it cost so much to keep running that they should have sold a daughter rather than married them off with dowries.

But they were hardly destitute. They had servants, yet no footman had gone forward to answer the door. It was most odd.

The third time the knocking resumed, Maria glanced instinctively at her father, who sighed heavily.

"My dear," he said mildly to his wife, "I believe we have so few servants about the place that there is no one to answer the door."

Leonora held her head high, and Maria smiled despite herself. There was no one like her mother for refusing to accept any criticism, even if it was kindly and gently meant.

"I have no idea what you mean," Leonora said icily as the knocking continued, echoing around the room.

Kitty snorted. "We'll have to send one of the menfolk out."

"Kitty!" said Isabella, scandalized. "We cannot send Papa to answer his own door!"

"I'll go," said Isaac, rising to his feet. "'Tis no trouble."

"No, this is ridiculous, there must be someone else," said Olivia haughtily, and Maria stifled a laugh. Since she had become Lady Kingsley, a few things had rather gone to her sister's head. "I will ring the bell and—"

"Don't ring the bell!" Kitty said with a giggle. "You want to give the few servants we still have even more to do?"

The chatter spilled out, people speaking over each other, half listening, speaking louder and louder to have their voices heard, but instead, only contributing to the cacophony.

Maria's heart twisted, her head hurting with all the noise. She always hated the rambunctious nature of her sisters; it was unkind to think such things, but she wished they could quiet their voices a little.

As it was…

"No, listen!" Kitty almost shouted, standing so she could square up to Olivia. "In my opinion…"

They were all speaking so loudly, in fact, Tommy joining in with the yelling though, he had no comprehension what the conversation was about, that no one noticed Maria rise from her chair, stride across the room, and slip out into the hall.

She leaned against the closed door with relief. The sound was muffled now, though the knocking on the front door was louder. Who could it be? Who could be disturbing them this close to Christmas? It had to be important, or why else knock so loudly and so insistently?

Well, there was only one way to stop that.

Striding forward with far more bravery than she felt, Maria grasped the door handle and pulled it open.

"Yes?" she asked in as icy a tone as she could manage, channeling her mother's elegant aloofness. "What do you…you…"

Maria swallowed. Her tongue had entirely gotten away from her, but then it always did when there was a handsome man in her presence, and this gentleman was perhaps the most handsome she had ever seen.

Tall. Taller than her, which was saying something. Her Papa had always described her as the gangly one of his four daughters. But not just tall, but…proud. Determined. There was something in the eyes, a confidence Maria recognized in others, even if she had never experienced it herself.

A man who knew what he wanted. Windswept hair and a rather dashing coat, with a woolen knitted scarf around his shoulders, in the dying afternoon light he was lit up from behind and appeared to glow. Like an angel. A Christmas angel.

The gentleman smiled, and Maria's stomach lurched. Like a devil. Like a handsome man designed to tempt her.

"You…" she repeated, hardly knowing what she was saying.

And it was nonsense. She did not know him. Maria did not believe she had ever seen him before in her life.

Yet she was captivated. Here was a man whose attentions she would gratefully receive.

Not that he would ever think of her. Indeed, he was looking at her right now with a slightly confused expression, as though he could not understand what she was saying.

Maria managed to close her mouth and swallowed hard. *She* had no idea what she was saying. Oh, trust her to make a complete fool of herself the moment she encountered such a handsome man.

"Hullo," said the gentleman with a grin. "You're a funny looking maid."

Heat seated Maria's cheeks. Maid? Maid! He thought her a servant, in her own home? The outrage! The absolute indignity of it! Surely he could see by the quality of her gown that she was a daughter of the house—the blaggard!

Though these words were clear and concise in her mind, Maria found when she opened her mouth, the only sound that came out was, "Ahhhh…"

Oh, it was all too bad, Maria thought wretchedly. She never had any chance of attracting him, whoever he was, once he met Isabella. But still. It would have been pleasant, for a few minutes, to have a rational conversation with a handsome man.

As it was…

"Or, not a maid," the gentleman said, his grin widening, making his features all the more pleasant in the late afternoon sun. "I have offended you with my quip, I do apologize."

Maria took a deep breath. Well, she had made an utter fool of herself already, so there was no point in hoping to impress the man. She may as well speak directly to him, as she would any other servant.

"I am not offended," she said, completely falsely. "Maria Fitzroy."

"Walter Arborn," came the polite response with a nod of his

head. "I have taken the cottage by the vicarage for the Christmas season."

Maria's curiosity, already piqued, only increased at this scant information.

Walter Arborn. She had never heard of him before, and the name was not one familiar to her. A stranger, then. A stranger in Chalcroft village just before Christmas—and taking the vicarage cottage, that was interesting. The gossip around the vicar letting the place had been quite substantial, but no one had any details on the person to whom it was let.

And now he was standing before her. Walter Arborn. Mr. Arborn, she supposed she should call him.

"Well, Mr. Arborn," Maria said as haughtily as she could manage, "I hope you have a pleasant Christmas Season."

Walter's eyes flickered over her. "Oh, I think I will. I certainly think I will."

Heat flushed through Maria's body. There was but a mere hint of a suggestion in the gentleman's voice, but it was enough.

He was—was he flirting with her? What a strange thing indeed! No one flirted with her, the youngest of the Fitzroy sisters. Not when there was any other Fitzroy sister to speak to, at least.

But this gentleman...he was looking at her as though he...*well*. As though he liked what he saw. His smile had never disappeared, not since she had first opened the door, but it had changed somehow. Deepened.

Maria could not have explained it, even if she had wanted to. The idea of ever describing to someone what she felt when Walter Arborn looked at her...no. It could not be borne. She would never do it.

"I should have known a lady so beautiful would not be a maid," said Walter softly, taking a step toward her. "You are a Fitzroy, of course. One of the beautiful Fitzroys I have heard so much about, and I should have guessed you were Maria. The most beautiful."

Maria swallowed. It was a nonsense, of course. He was lying.

At the very least, jesting. No one had ever described her in such a way, not even her own mother.

But to hear those words from his lips…

Hot and cold at the same time. Tingles all over her body. As though she needed to be close to him, needed him to touch her…

Maria blanched at the very thought, but she could not help staring at the handsome man. It was not seemly for a young lady to have such thoughts—indeed, she had never really had such thoughts before.

No man had ever been so enticing as to elicit them.

But she was no complete innocent, at least, she had never done any of the things she knew a man and a woman could enjoy together, but her mother had been most careful to ensure that each of her four daughters knew…well. The dangers of what a gentleman could offer.

Not that Maria had ever been in that sort of danger. Her gaze flickered over Walter, the square of his jaw, just a little stubble there as though he had not shaved in a few days. Traveling, probably. His broad shoulders, the strength in his hands, she could see without needing to touch them.

Oh, to be touched by those hands…

"I wanted to speak to your mother."

Maria blinked. So lost she had become in her thoughts, she had quite forgotten Walter Arborn was still standing before her—and was watching her examine him.

"M-My mother?" she repeated, hardly certain whether she had heard him correctly.

Walter nodded cheerfully. "Yes, your mother—Mrs. William Fitzroy?"

"I know who my mother is," Maria found herself saying foolishly.

He laughed, as though she had intentionally been witty, and a smile crept over Maria's face weakly as she laughed with him.

Oh, this was glorious. No wonder Isabella wished to go to Bath, meet gentlemen, flirt with them ever so slightly across a crowded room or while dancing or listening to a recital.

Joy was flooding her heart as it never had before. To be with a gentleman, and for him to look at her like that, as though she was genuinely amusing…it was wonderful. It was everything. Everything she wanted.

"Yes, I rather thought you would know her," said Walter easily with a grin. "I—well, I wanted to ask her something, as I was so new to the neighborhood, and I thought she might be able to…"

His voice trailed off delicately, and Maria smiled, heart thumping a little painfully. Walter wanted to see her mother—and that would bring him into the house, to spend more time with her. It was a marvelous idea.

"Of course," Maria said, her smile shy yet determined. She pulled open the front door to allow him entrance. "I think my mother is—"

"My wife is not available for visitors."

Maria looked round and saw her father standing just behind her, a rather strange look on his face. He was staring at Walter as though the man had done him a great injury, which did not make sense.

Why, she had never met Walter before, and she was certain her father did not know him. So how could he be looking at him with such a glare, an ire that was typically reserved for those who had done wrong?

Maria glanced back round at Walter, who seemed unperturbed by the direct statement.

"Such a shame. I will return another time—if there is a more convenient time Mrs. Fitzroy would—"

"No," said William roughly. "I am afraid not. Good day, sir."

Maria could do nothing, say nothing—there was no time. By the time she had collected her wits about her, the door had been closed right in Walter's face, and she was left staring at the wood, wondering in her heart whether he was standing on the other side, staring at the other side of the door.

Wishing, as she was, that it was not there.

"Maria, do you know that man?"

Maria turned to look at her father. She had never seen such a strange expression on his face, not fear exactly, but something close to it. Akin to dread, yet not the thing itself.

She shook her head. In this moment of longing, wishing Walter was inside rather than outside, she was not certain she trusted her own voice.

Her father sighed heavily. "Good, good. Well, if he comes to the front door again, you are not to let him in, you understand?"

Perhaps if Maria had been Kitty or any of her sisters, she would have asked why. Who was the man, what did he want with her mother, and why was she to forbid him entrance into the house?

But she was not her sisters. Her bravery did not extend that far.

"Of course, Papa," Maria said meekly.

He nodded, saying nothing more, and returned to the drawing room.

Maria sighed and leaned against the door. Walter Arborn. Who was he? Why had he wished to see her mother, and why had her father taken against him so?

And far more importantly, how was she ever to forget such a man?

CHAPTER TWO

THE AIR WAS bracing as Maria stepped out into the frozen morning. Snow had fallen heavily in the night, covering Chalcroft, its gardens, and parklands with at least three inches of delicate, white snow.

It had looked beautiful from Maria's bedchamber window, and the moment she had pulled back the curtains, she had been determined to go for a ride.

Get out of the house full of people and noise and chatter, constant demands on her attention for conversation or watching her nephews…

Get away from it all.

Maria sighed happily as she closed the side door behind her and trudged across to the stables, her riding boots crunching in the snow.

Breakfast had been a rather busy affair, plenty of chatter between her sisters, her two brothers-in-law seated together and talking away about something Maria had not found interesting, and it had taken her mother two attempts to gain her attention to pass the butter.

Her mind had been…elsewhere. With someone else.

Maria's cheeks were pink with the cold, she was sure, and nothing else. At least, that was what she told herself as she opened the door to the stable and smiled at her mare, Storm.

There could be no other reason for her cheeks to turn such a scalding color. It certainly could not be because she had spent most of the evening and half the night thinking about a certain someone.

A certain gentleman who had looked at her as though she was…astounding. As though she was precisely what he had been looking for.

As though Walter had come to Chalcroft just for her.

"You are a Fitzroy, of course. One of the beautiful Fitzroys I have heard so much about, and I should have guessed you were Maria. The most beautiful."

Maria sighed heavily. She was being ridiculous. Walter Arborn—Mr. Arborn, as she should think of him—had certainly not come to Chalcroft to see her. He'd come to see her mother, which made little sense. What could a gentleman from…had he mentioned where he had come from?…want with her mother?

Still, the point was that he had not come to see *her*.

Maria tried to distract herself with the tack and saddle for her mare, who stood patiently and allowed Maria to ready her for a ride.

The thing to do, Maria told herself sternly as she mounted her horse, *was to completely put Mr. Arborn out of her mind.*

She would never see him again, not properly, and she would certainly not have a chance to speak with him alone. He had flattered her, yes, but that was all it was. Flattery. She should certainly not allow his words to sink into her heart, creating expectations which he could never fulfill.

"I should have guessed you were Maria. The most beautiful."

"Do not be ridiculous," Maria said under her breath as she encouraged Storm forward out of the stable and into the freezing air. "Walter Arborn is not here for you, and he is certainly not going to be impressed by your nonsense. Ignore him. Forget him!"

It was hard to do. As Maria rode her horse through Chalcroft Farm and toward the woodland, where some of the most spectacular rides could be enjoyed, she could not force the image of Walter's smile from her mind.

He was a mightily handsome man, she had to admit.

The woods were very still. The snow wasn't so thick here, the heavy branches over Maria's head were leafless yet had still prevented much snow falling to the ground as she rode along. But there was a stillness and a silence that only winter, and in Maria's mind, only winter near Christmas, could give.

She breathed out very slowly, allowing her shoulders to slump a little. There was something about being alone that allowed her to be completely herself.

"Maria Fitzroy."

Maria's head jerked to the left where the voice—a voice she recognized, though she had only heard it for the first time yesterday—had come from. Her hands jerked, too, the reins in her fingers tightening, and her mare halted suddenly.

Heart fluttering painfully, Maria saw Walter Arborn leaning against a tree, one foot against the trunk, with a knowing smile on his face.

Walter Arborn. What was he doing here? Maria's chest tightened as her heart pounded a little more quickly, her mind in a rush of confusion.

Why, it was as though she had dreamt him up from her head, as though her continuous thoughts about Walter, thoughts she certainly should not be having, had somehow managed to draw him to her.

Maria swallowed and felt relieved, in that moment, that she was astride a horse and could not stumble and make a fool of herself by tripping over. Though of course, it was perfectly possible for her to make a fool of herself in an entirely different way…

"Walter," she said, without thinking.

Walter's smile did not become broader, exactly, but there was a shift in his face, and it made Maria's stomach lurch most painfully.

Goodness, he was handsome. Well-featured, as her mother might say. Divine, as Isabella would say.

All Maria knew was that her knees were weak, and her hands warm in her gloves, and the cold wintery wind, which had been chilling her, seemed to have died away.

What was he doing here?

"I hoped I would run into you," said Walter easily, still leaning against the tree. "I thought if I were to meet anyone, it would be you."

Maria's throat went dry. *What did he mean by it? What did he hope to gain by saying such a thing?*

And she was alone. With Walter, that was. Maria had never been to London, but she and her family had been to Bath often. At least once a year. She knew the social decorum as well as any other young lady of the *ton*, and she knew it was most scandalous to be alone with a gentleman one was not related to.

But…well. This was Chalcroft. The countryside.

Those sorts of rules were more difficult to maintain when in the countryside, when long walks alone were the only solace a lady could find when the world was too dull to bear.

"I did not think I would see you," Maria said honestly, the words slipping from her mouth before she could make them more impressive.

That was certainly not what Olivia would have said—or Kitty. Kitty would have been haughty, impressive. She was, after all, now married to the son of a duke.

But Walter did not appear to mind. Something danced in his eyes, approval, perhaps. At the very least, he did not seem surprised nor offended at the baldness of her words.

"But I am a welcome sight, I hope?"

Maria felt her cheeks pink and hoped beyond hope he would merely believe it to be a symptom of the cold winter day.

It was certainly not because she was impressed by him. Certainly not. Not in the slightest.

"Yes," she said, hardly aware of what she was saying. "I

mean—"

"Here, let me help you," said Walter, moving away from the tree and toward her with his hand outstretched.

For a moment, the smallest of moments, Maria hesitated. She was not the horsewoman Isabella was and would find it difficult to dismount Storm with no mounting block.

Besides, lowering herself meant getting close to Walter. Closer than was appropriate.

For some reason, this thought did not increase her hesitation but instead spurred her on. Maria let go of the reins and took Walter's hand, gently letting herself slide from the mare to the ground.

And he was close. Too close. She had not realized just how close he was until she had descended, and now she had his chest before her and Storm behind her, and there was nowhere for her to go. She looked up into Walter's eyes and saw—something. Greed. Hunger. Desire.

Maria's lips parted, unbidden, at the heady thoughts that shot through her mind. Of Walter lowering his head and kissing her, his lips touching hers, feeling the strength of him as she clung to—

"Well, Maria, I do not think you could have chosen a better day for your ride," said Walter cheerfully, letting go of her hand and stepping away from her so quickly, Maria felt her breath pulled from her lungs.

He was gone. His presence, so intoxicating, so masculine, had disappeared.

He was walking slowly along the path, and Maria almost tripped over her feet—as she had known she would—to walk alongside him.

"A better day?"

Walter raised his arms expressively. "Glorious winter weather, do not you think?"

Maria nodded, hardly able to think. *She was on an unchaperoned walk with a gentleman she did not know.*

At least, Storm did not count as much of a chaperone. The mare was following behind obediently, well trained, and this meant Maria could focus all her attention on the man beside her.

The man who was making her body feel something rather wild and indelicate.

"Yes, I was told the winters here around Chalcroft were most beautiful," continued Walter, not requiring Maria to contribute to the conversation, for which she was most grateful. "Beautiful woodlands, a quiet cottage…beautiful women…"

Maria swallowed. His hands had fallen to his sides now, which meant that her hand was right beside his. If he shifted slightly on the path; if she moved slightly closer…

"And is—is that why you are here?" Maria heard herself ask.

Walter glanced at her. "What do you mean?"

It did not seem to be a difficult question, but Maria attempted to elaborate over the heavy thumping of her heart. "Here at Chalcroft. At the vicar's cottage, is that why you took it for the Christmas season?"

There was a knowing smile on Walter's face. "For the beautiful women?"

"F-For the woodlands."

What had possessed her to even attempt to make conversation with such an attractive man? Maria should have known better than to even try to appear respectable and interesting.

She should have nodded her head and continued on by when she had seen Walter by the tree. That would have been the wise thing to do.

Walter, however, did not appear to think that she had said anything foolish at all.

Quite the contrary, he nodded as their footsteps crunched on the snowy ground. "Yes, a change of air. London, as you know, is so dirty, so crowded in the winter, Christmas especially. I wanted to get away, see some of the Christmas traditions of the countryside."

Maria nodded, as though she knew London well and had not

just heard of it from her London Fitzroy cousins. "Christmas traditions. Yes."

She really should leave. Maria could hear herself speaking, knew she was saying nothing of interest, and, in fact, was making herself look more like a fool of a chit than a respectable young lady.

But she could not leave him. Walter, whoever he was, drew her to him like a moth to a flame. Like the geese fly south for winter, there was an instinct in her that told her this Walter Arborn was a good man.

A man worth knowing.

"Yes, we have plenty of traditions here at Chalcroft during the festive season," Maria said, doing her best to sound as nonchalant as her mother. "The church is decorated, of course, and there is a pudding made for the poor and in one part of it—"

"And what about Fitzroy Christmas traditions?" Walter said, cutting across her. "I would dearly love to hear of some of your family traditions. Would perhaps like to celebrate them with you if I may."

Maria almost tripped over a stone, heart plummeting, skirts flying as she fell to the ground—but strong hands had grasped her hand and swung her upright—right into the arms of Walter Arborn.

"Careful now," said Walter quietly, his arms around Maria's waist as she tried desperately to catch her breath. "You might hurt yourself."

Maria looked up into Walter's eyes, felt the scalding heat of his hands on her waist, her stomach lurching, her heart beating so fast, she was almost sure it was a hum, and knew she was about to be very hurt.

For this would not end how she hoped. This sort of thing happened to…to anyone but her. To Kitty, when she had met Isaac and fallen in love with him in just a week. To their cousin Harmony, who had been wooed and wed by David in just a few weeks.

Those men had seen something in her cousin and sister she simply did not have.

Which meant it was even more inexplicable that Walter was looking at her...*well. Like that.* As though she was truly interesting. Captivating.

His gaze flickered to her lips, and Maria found herself licking them.

Something akin to a groan emitted from Walter's lips. "Maria..."

Maria wrenched herself from Walter's arms, taking a few steps back for good measure. This was ridiculous. She was seeing things that weren't there, and worse of all, so was he.

Once he got to know her, once he actually spoke to her for more than five minutes, Walter—Mr. Arborn—would see there was nothing special about her. She was just a Fitzroy, and though they were an impressive family, she was nothing important within it.

That was what she needed to do, Maria told herself firmly as she smoothed down her skirts and picked off an imaginary piece of dust. *Just talk.* He would soon see she was not worth the attention and leave her alone.

"Yes, we have many Christmas customs," said Maria, trying to calm her voice into her natural tones rather than the tense croak she was managing now. "We have Christmas wreaths, wreaths that we make ourselves."

Though she had taken a step as though to continue their walk along the path, there appeared to be something wrong with Walter. The man was shaking his head slowly, as though trying to rid it of water.

"Mr. Arborn?"

Walter caught her eye. "I much preferred it when you called me Walter."

Maria swallowed. She was not going to convince herself this was something special, special to her. Mr. Arborn obviously was accustomed to a lighter formality than she was. That was all.

This was not for her.

"Well, Mr. Arborn," she said with a small smile as she continued along the path, "the Christmas wreaths go all over the house, almost every door has one."

Footsteps. They matched the heavy patter of her heart, and Maria forced herself not to glance at Walter as he joined her on the path, her horse still following them.

"And do you make a Christmas wreath?"

Maria nodded. "Olivia is the best—my eldest sister—but as she is married now, it is left rather up to myself and Bels to—"

"And where does this Christmas tradition come from?" asked Walter, eagerness dripping from his voice. "From your mother, perhaps?"

There was nothing in his words specifically that made Maria hesitate; it was more a sense. A feeling.

It was her mother Walter had wanted to see yesterday, and her father had sent him away most rudely. And now Walter had met with her—accidently, of course, there was no possibility he could have planned it—and was asking about her mother again.

"I…what do you want to know about my mother?" Maria asked awkwardly.

As she looked at Walter, something changed. The light went out of his eyes, his interest immediately gone, and he looked away from her, back the way they had come.

"Well, I had better go," he said in a dull tone of finality. "Good day, Miss Fitzroy."

Walter started walking away from her.

Maria stood, indecision wracking her mind as she tried to think, not to feel—feel the desperate loneliness of being without him. She had only been in his company nigh on ten minutes, and already the world felt lesser, empty, without him. As though she had something precious and had then immediately lost it.

Walter was walking away, and she hated that. She wanted him to stay. Maria could not have described it—a strange sense within her that only when Walter was with her was the world as it should be.

"Wait!"

Walter halted, twisting to look at her with a raised eyebrow. "Yes?"

Maria thought quickly, trying to push all concern prickling around the edges of her heart away.

It could not hurt to tell him a little about the family, could it? It was just Christmas traditions; there was no harm in that. The whole village knew about them. It was hardly a secret. Why should her Papa be concerned with that?

"The Christmas wreaths are a Fitzroy tradition," she said quietly, eyes fixed on Walter. "Not my mother's family."

In an instant, it was as though whatever breach between them had been mended. Walter beamed, striding forward to return to her side.

"So, what are your mother's Christmas traditions?" he asked softly.

Maria looked up at him, a mere foot away, and wished she was brave enough to close the gap, remove the distance between them. Find herself in his arms again.

"My…my mother gives special gifts to the servants," she said with a shy smile. "She spends almost all autumn on them—handmade things, you know, made for each servant."

Walter nodded. "Now that is something special."

"I think the servants look forward to them all year," said Maria with a small laugh. "Though it might be the gift of five pounds she includes in each one!"

"Five pounds?" repeated Walter, and Maria nodded. "How generous."

Maria nodded, heart soaring. It was wonderful to share this small part of her family's Christmas habits with him. Oh, if only…but now, it was a foolish thing to even hope for. Walter would not be spending Christmas with the Fitzroys.

Though he was all alone in that cottage, a small part of Maria whispered. *All alone, and at Christmas!* Why not invite him to stay with you—there is plenty of room at Chalcroft.

"Do...do you wish to continue our walk?" Maria asked timidly.

For a heart-stopping moment, she was certain he was going to accept her invitation, but—

"Alas, I cannot," said Walter, and he truly did look regretful at his departure. "Another time, Maria."

Maria shivered at the sound of her name on his lips. It was most scandalous to be sure, yet she liked it. She could not pretend she did not.

"Miss Fitzroy," she breathed.

Walter smiled and pushed back a curl from her face. Just the simplest act of his fingers brushing against her face was enough to make Maria's stomach lurch and warmth grow between her legs.

"I like Maria," he said softly. "Until next time."

CHAPTER THREE

"MARIA?"

Maria jumped. The entire breakfast table was staring at her, as though she had sprouted a second head.

Embarrassment shot through her at the realization that so many people were looking at her. *This was the trouble with families,* she thought bitterly, though she would never express it. She liked each of them individually. It was only when forced to confront all at once that she wondered what it would be like to be an only child.

"Yes?" she said defensively to Olivia, who had spoken her name.

Olivia raised an eyebrow. "I said, please pass the butter. How many times must I say it before you heed me?"

Maria swallowed. She had not heard her sister's request.

That was the trouble with allowing one's mind to wander at the breakfast table. She was not exactly a morning person at the best of times, unlike her sisters, and when one's mind was entirely preoccupied with a handsome gentleman with whom you had spent a few secret moments, yet who had completely captured your heart, one was wont to accidently not hear things.

"I do not know what is wrong with you today, Maria," said Kitty with a shake of her head. "Or yesterday, now I come to think of it, or the day before. You've returned from your rides in a most strange temper."

Maria's gaze dropped to her plate of potatoes and eggs but said nothing.

What could she say? That she had spent a little time with a charming man who called her Maria, caught her before falling, called her beautiful?

That she had been unable to think, unable to do anything, since that moment? Though it had now been two days since she had first seen Walter, it did not matter, because every time she closed her eyes, she could see his face? The way his eyebrows met when he frowned, the way a dimple appeared in his right cheek when he laughed?

"Maria, for goodness' sake, the butter!"

Maria almost jumped in her seat, her sister's words were so abrupt—but then, it appeared she had been pushed beyond all endurance. There were heavy bags under her sister's eyes and lines around her mouth that Maria had never seen before. A newborn was far more difficult than she could suppose.

Olivia's husband, Luke, put a hand on her arm. "Let me get it for you, my dear."

Rising from the table, he reached over to pick up the butter dish and brought it over to his wife.

Maria smiled awkwardly at Olivia, who did not smile back. Well, it was tiring, she had heard, being a mother. She supposed she could not hold it against her sister if she was so unreasonable.

Their father snorted loudly from behind his newspaper.

Leonora smiled indulgently. "The news giving you grief, my dear?"

Maria picked up her knife and fork and started to eat as her father snorted again. It was not like him to be so affronted by the news of the day—but then, her Papa was never one to let his opinion be hidden.

"Grief? Grief? I'll give them grief," said her father most unexpectedly.

Maria looked up and saw instantly she was not the only one.

Everyone around the breakfast table looked up at William Fitzroy, who was clearly in a storming temper—something none of them had ever seen.

William put down the newspaper in a heap on the breakfast table and glared at it, as though it had personally offended him.

"Goodness, what is all this about?" Maria found herself asking.

Now the entire table was looking at her with almost as much surprise. Maria pressed her lips together, hardly sure how she had managed to find the bravery to speak so boldly.

What had got into her?

"This, this article—no, I will not give it such credence, 'tis a slander!" said her Papa, and the table turned back to him. "It is an outrage! It is offensive! I shall write to my solicitor!"

Maria's stomach twisted painfully. *What on earth could be in the newspaper that was so injudicious? Something that her father believed to be…about them?*

"Listen to this," said William with a growl in his voice. "This nonsense, I do not know who they get to write these sorts of things…"

He picked up the newspaper with bad grace and flicked through the pages to find the item which had so insulted him.

"Right, here we are…lots of guff about Christmas, about how to treat one's servants during the festive season, additional responsibilities, blah blah blah…yes, here it is. 'Mrs. William Fitzroy, of Chalcroft, however, takes a very different view than we expect of most of our readers. She offers her servants but one gift a year, at Yuletide, forcing her servants to wait all year for a gift, which she has not even bothered to purchase herself.' The cheek of it!"

Maria glanced quickly at her mother.

Who would write such a thing? It was untrue, for a start. Her mother gave gifts to the servants on her birthday, their birthdays, and at Easter and Michaelmas.

"Do not credit it, Mama," said Olivia hastily, looking over at their mother. "The scoundrel, I will not do him the honor of calling him a journalist, clearly does not know you."

"He certainly does not, and I shall make sure that the man pays for it," grumbled their father, throwing the newspaper onto the floor in a heap rather than attempt to refold the thing. "The cheek! The very idea!"

"Do not worry yourself about it, William," said Leonora, head held high, though Maria could see the hurt in her eyes. "'Tis a nonsense. I am sure anyone who knows me—"

"Maria, you'll be watching little Tommy this morning, won't you?"

Distracted from her mother's words, Maria looked over at Olivia, who had made the bold declaration.

"Won't you?" Olivia said hopefully.

Maria opened her mouth, thought better of it, and closed it again. It was not as though she was particularly averse to caring for her nephew. He was a darling boy and such a departure from the many Fitzroy sisters and cousins that the entire family doted on him.

Still...

Maria's eyes darted over to the window, despite herself. Yesterday had snowed so heavily it had been impossible to even think about going outside, but today was bright, crisp, the snow from the last few days still lying on the ground.

A perfect day for a ride.

Her stomach lurched painfully, and she was forced to admit to herself it was not precisely a ride that she was hoping for. More the presence of a certain gentleman...

"Oh no, Maria cannot help you with Tommy this morning," said Isabella lightly.

Olivia turned to her sister. "Why on earth not?"

"She is helping me with Christmas wreaths," said Isabella, utterly unperturbed by her sister's glare. "There are still so many to do, and I honestly do not believe I will be able to do them all myself. You'll help me, won't you, Maria?"

Maria smiled weakly at both of her sisters. "I..."

Why could she not say what she wanted? Why was it so difficult to speak her mind?

It had never been a problem for any of her sisters, inheriting their father's desire for clarity and their mother's fiery temper, none of them had ever minced their words.

It was only Maria who found it nigh on impossible to speak her mind. *And that was why,* she thought dully, *instead of going for a ride, escaping the household, and hopefully catching a glimpse of Walter—if she was so bold as to ride by the vicarage and the cottage— she would be trapped here.* Caring for a little one or making wreaths, neither as appealing as her wish.

"I..." Maria tried to speak, but the words did not come out. Her gaze dropped to the brooch she had chosen that morning, a Christmas wreath. No wonder Kitty wished for her assistance.

"Why don't you get Tommy involved in the wreathmaking this year?" Luke said with a grin at both his wife and Isabella. "Is it not nigh on time for the little one to get involved in Fitzroy Christmas traditions?"

"Oh, that would be lovely," said Olivia, clapping her hands with delight.

Maria noticed Kitty roll her eyes and tried to stifle a smile. Kitty had never been much one for getting entirely into the Christmas spirit.

"Where are the materials for the wreaths? We always used to do it in the gun room, but when I passed by yesterday..."

As Maria watched the conversation meander between her sisters, she rose very slowly, very quietly, from her chair. She had slipped out of the breakfast room before anyone asked her where she was going, and within twenty minutes, she had on her riding habit and gloves, and was striding out toward the stables as though she was following orders.

She was not taking the same path as before because she hoped to meet Walter. At least, that was what Maria tried to tell herself. Her heart tightened at the thought of seeing him again, this man who had entirely taken over all her waking thoughts.

Was this what falling in love was like?

For the first time, as Maria mounted Storm and encouraged her out of the stables and toward the woods, she wished she had asked her sisters what it had been like, falling in love. It was just a conversation they had never had. Neither had she asked about…well…

Her cheeks flushed in the cool morning air. Maria tried not to think about all the things she had dreamt about last night. Kisses and touches and wildness she could never hope to enjoy.

Certainly not with Walter. Why, chances were he was in the cottage he had rented, by the fire, enjoying a good book and—

"We really have to stop meeting like this," said Walter with a smile as she turned a corner to find him walking along the path toward Chalcroft. "As the goose flies south, I seem to fly to you."

A slow smile crept across Maria's face, and this time, she did nothing to attempt to hide it. Why should she? It was impossible to prevent anyone seeing just how much she enjoyed Walter's company, least of all stop Walter from noticing.

She wanted him to notice. *To notice her.*

"Good morning, Mr. Arborn," Maria managed to say as she slipped from her horse without waiting for Walter to offer his hand.

The fewer opportunities she had for looking like a fool for wanting to be close to him, the better, she told herself. Even if it was sad to miss a chance to be so close. Feel his warmth.

"Walter," said Walter as he offered her his arm. "I wish you would call me Walter. Shall we?"

Maria hesitated only for a moment. Why, it was a walk, nothing more. They were on the footpath, anyone could come across them, there was nothing indecorous about going for a walk.

And it was not as though they had planned this.

A shiver rushed through her heart. Even if she had hoped for it. Even if she had wished it more than anything.

"I hope you were not too bored yesterday," she said quietly

as they began to walk slowly along the path. "With all the snow, I mean."

"I was not bored, no," Walter said quietly. "I had…well. Something on my mind that kept me quite preoccupied. Someone."

Maria's breath caught in her throat, but she forced herself to ignore it. She would not permit herself to be so overwhelmed. Walter could certainly not mean *her*.

"Oh?" she said as lightly as she could manage.

The path came to a fork, the left swiftly became Chalcroft Farm, right by the house itself, and the right meandering away, deeper into the woodland.

Maria's thoughts scattered, trying desperately to think which she should take. It would be highly suggestive if she invited him to Chalcroft—and besides, her father's words were still ringing in her ears.

"Well, if he comes to the front door again, you are not to let him in, you understand?"

But to suggest the right-hand path was to suggest an intimacy she and Walter did not have—a longer walk together, further from prying eyes.

Which to take?

As it turned out, Maria did not need to decide. Walter carefully but decisively steered her toward the right-hand path.

"You do not mind a longer walk with me, do you?" he asked quietly.

Maria swallowed and shook her head, not trusting her voice.

"These woods are beautiful," Walter said with a heavy sigh as their footsteps crunched on the snow. "There is nothing like this in London, where I grew up."

"I know nothing different, I suppose, but I must admit they are beautiful, even in winter," Maria confessed, her heart racing.

But not as beautiful as you, she wanted to say. *They do not take my breath away as they do you. They do not strike me almost dumb with their presence, stop me thinking as you do…*

"Your father must know them very well, having grown up here," said Walter lightly. "And your mother? Where is she from?"

There it was again. Maria glanced up at Walter, as though she could discern his purpose by a mere look. His face was just as handsome as ever and gave her no indication why such questions were being asked.

It was most confusing. Why, Maria loved her mother dearly, of course, but there was nothing particularly remarkable about her—about any of them.

"I don't know," Maria said hesitantly. "At least, Italy. Beyond that I cannot say."

Walter's eyes met hers, and Maria almost gasped. They were no longer walking. She was not sure how or why they had stopped. But they were standing in the middle of the path, her arm in his, and he was looking at her.

Maria had never been looked at like that by...by anyone. It was intoxicating. As though he had pinned her to the earth with his gaze, preventing her from moving.

Not that she would move even if she could. Why, standing here, in the still wintery silence with Walter...there was nowhere else Maria wanted to be.

"I like your brooch."

Maria blinked. Walter had said something—at least, his lips had moved, and she was fairly sure he had said something.

What he had said, she had no idea.

"Your brooch," murmured Walter. He had released her arm now, but though Maria had worried about him stepping away from her, he was somehow closer. Standing right before her, his hand brushing the brooch visible at the neck of her pelisse, a wreath of holly. "A Fitzroy wreath."

Maria smiled helplessly. She was helpless when in Walter's presence, his intense masculinity overpowering her in a way she did not understand. In a way she could not explain.

"Yes," she breathed. "Yes, a Fitzroy Christmas wreath."

A strange look overcame Walter's eyes, and in that moment, Maria knew what was about to happen, though she did not know how.

Walter moved forward, suddenly, as though unable to restrain himself any longer, and his lips were on hers, and Maria moaned at the intensity of it.

Her first kiss. No chaste, delicate thing, no peck on the lips that would be over as soon as she realized it was happening.

Oh no, this was something else entirely. Dark and dangerous and unrestrained. Walter's hands were on her waist, griping her tight, pulling her into his chest, and his lips took possession of her own. Maria's moan had partly opened her lips, and Walter took advantage, his tongue ravishing her own, questing forth, sparking pleasure that radiated through her body, and Maria fell into his arms as desire overwhelmed her.

Her fingers were somehow curled in his hair, his top hat fallen to the ground, and Maria knew she would never be able to kiss anyone else like this, never. Not now she had tasted Walter, tasted his desire, his desperation for her—where it came from, she could not think, but it did not matter.

Thinking was not the important thing now. Feeling was all that mattered.

Walter nibbled gently on her bottom lip, and Maria's head fell back, her mind overwhelmed with the sensations—and then she moaned as his lips found her neck, grazing against skin, until he placed a delicate kiss on her collarbone.

"Maria…" he whispered.

It was enough to startle Maria back into her senses.

Heat rushed to her face at the realization of what she had done, of the compromising position she had permitted herself to be put in. Maria removed her hands from Walter's neck—most regretfully—and pushed him away.

"We—we should not have…we cannot…" she said, hardly knowing where to look.

At least, Maria knew where she wanted to look. When she

could eventually manage to look at Walter, there was a wry smile on his face as he shook his head.

"Damn, I am sorry, Maria," he whispered.

Maria's stomach dropped. *Of course he was sorry.* There was no possibility he could truly have meant to do that—perhaps he was leaning forward to brush a leaf from her hair, and she had got entirely the wrong idea.

It was mortifying. She would never live it down. She would have to stay inside Chalcroft and never leave the place until Walter had gone back to London. Perhaps even longer than that…

"Do not be," she said heavily, dropping her gaze to the snow-strewn forest floor.

But a hand reached forward and tilted up her chin. Maria looked into the serious eyes of Walter and saw something there…something she had never seen before.

It was more than desire, it was…*interest.*

"I am sorry because I had promised myself not to kiss you until much further into our acquaintance," said Walter seriously, "not because I am sorry I kissed you."

Maria swallowed, heat flushing into her cheeks, but she managed to hold his gaze. "Oh."

"Oh indeed," Walter said darkly. "Oh dear. If I was attracted to you less…well. There it is."

He dropped his hand, and Maria stood there, hardly knowing what to do next. *He was attracted to her? Surely not.*

But then, he had said it—and Walter had certainly kissed as though he was a man with a deep-rooted desire.

She had never believed herself likely to be in such a situation, but she was. Now she had to decide what she was going to do about it.

She placed her arm in Walter's. "I believe you promised me a walk."

A slow smile crept across Walter's face. "I…I did indeed."

Maria's stomach seemed to return, though it was mightily

churning. What she was doing…it was a little disgraceful. She should not be kissing gentlemen alone in the woods! And she certainly should not then be going on clandestine walks with them.

But those rules were for other people, not her. Not Walter. Walter was different. He was… Maria would never have admitted this to anyone else, but he was hers. She knew that, somehow, deep inside herself.

The only question was, did he think the same?

"Well then," Maria said lightly. "A walk. A chance for us to talk more."

"I would like that."

What Maria would have liked was more kissing—but then, it would hardly be ladylike to admit it. "Tell me…tell me about yourself."

"What do you want to know?" asked Walter with a laugh.

"Everything."

CHAPTER FOUR

"H ERE?"

"No, I do not think so—perhaps a little to the left?"

"How much longer are you two going to spend getting that perfect?"

Maria watched with a quiet smile from the sofa as Olivia and Isabella turned to glare at their brother-in-law.

Isaac put up his hands in mock surrender and retreated to the pianoforte, where Kitty was playing a rather tuneless Christmas carol. "Just a question…"

Maria chuckled with the rest of the family as Olivia and Isabella turned once again to the Christmas wreath they were trying to affix to the drawing room door. It was the last one, and only a small twinge of guilt entered Maria's heart as she realized that this year, she had not created a single one.

Not that anyone had noticed. In fact, the last two days when she had slipped out of the house to meet Walter in the woods, walking or riding, always talking, sometimes stealing a quick kiss but never permitting themselves to sink into such heady pleasures as their first…

Each time, Maria had come back home and felt certain her sisters were going to notice the change in her. Her mother, certainly.

Yet, none of them had. It was as though falling in love, desperately and powerfully, did not change her appearance at all.

Maria picked at the hem of her sleeve, tugging at a loose thread she should really have sewn back in, rather than let fray further. She should not think that way, but she could not help it.

Not when her thoughts so easily turned to Walter. To the way he laughed, his whole head tipped back as though he could not restrain himself.

The way he looked at her when he asked her questions. He was perhaps the first gentlemen to…well. *Ever take an interest in her.*

Maria was not one to feel jealous of her sisters, but when one was the youngest, there was always already someone prettier, more talented on the pianoforte, more impressive with their embroidery…

It was just something she had become accustomed to. Except now, when it felt like the least strange thing in the world that Walter should wish to talk to her and go for long walks with her in the woodlands…

Maria hugged herself and tried to stop thinking about him, but it was impossible. Walter Arborn had entirely taken over her mind, her heart, and she did not care.

Even missing the traditions the Fitzroy family had enjoyed for so many years did not matter.

A strange sort of sensation did pool in her stomach, however. It was not guilt, not exactly. More like a sense that she should feel guilty.

Was it not wrong for her, in a way, to be spending so much time with a man whom she had only met a few days ago?

A man she would know, perhaps, for many years to come.

"There!" said Olivia triumphantly. "Perfect!"

Maria glanced up. The large wreath, all holly, berries, and red ribbon, had been carefully placed right in the center of the mantelpiece. The door, evidently, had been abandoned.

At least, right in the center from one angle, Maria was sure. From where she was sitting…

There came a snort from the pianoforte. "Not quite right, Livvy!"

Olivia turned on her heels to glare at her sister. "Kitty Emmett, if you are so clever—"

"I think perhaps we can leave it for today," said Isaac hastily, raising his hands between the two sisters as though he was refereeing a boxing match. "It is just a wreath."

Every Fitzroy in the room stared at him as though he were mad.

"*Just* a wreath?" said Isabella incredulously. "How long have you been part of this family?"

"Not long enough, clearly," grinned Luke from an armchair by the fire.

Laughter and protests rang out around the room, the noise increasing as arguments slipped over each other, and Maria rose without saying a word. Sometimes the noise just became too much. That was when it was easier to leave them to it.

Besides, Maria thought as she closed the side door behind her and wandered toward Chalcroft farm, *it was not as though she was needed there*. Being needed was not something she had ever felt, not really. Oh, she was expected to look after Tommy, but that was not the same. They had servants for most things, and little was expected of her, save to marry well.

And even then, Maria thought, *she was not entirely sure whether her parents expected that of her*. Two daughters married, and the Chalcroft home secured on little Tommy. It would not be required of her to marry.

Perhaps she would just end up a spinster, staying at home with her mother until they were both old and gray. A smile danced across her lips at the thought. It would be a long time before that happened, and if her feelings for Walter were in any way reciprocated...

But it was foolish to think of such things, Maria told herself sternly as she wandered around a barn and came across the goose pen, a bucket of feed just beyond the gate.

Maria picked up the bucket and thrust her hand into the feed, scattering it into the pen. She watched the geese flock toward the food, eagerly pushing each other aside, desperately attempting to get to the food as though it would be their last chance to ever eat again.

Maria's heart twisted painfully. Was Walter her first, only, last chance at happiness? They had spoken much, she felt as though she knew him better than almost anyone…but at no point had their conversation included their feelings for each other.

Besides, what could she say? It was impossible for her to even understand what she was feeling, let alone reveal it to another.

A movement, just out of the corner of her eye. Maria turned hastily, knowing she was doing nothing wrong but conscious that she was alone.

Her heartbeat increased at the sight of Walter Arborn picking his way through the farm, past the barn, toward her.

"Walter," Maria said, a smile breaking out across her face.

Oh, it was wonderful to see him. She had given up all hope of seeing him today—she could not continue to take long walks alone—her sisters had mentioned enough times how irritated they were that she kept going out without them.

But to find him in the family farm, where she could talk to him with no concern about being in the wrong place…

"Maria," said Walter quietly as he reached her, placing his hands on the fence around the pen but looking directly at her.

All the tension in her shoulders at the approach of a stranger melted away, but Maria could not pretend there was not still a small amount of concern in her heart as she stood beside him.

Regardless of how comfortable she was around him, she had only met him a week ago. True, there were matches made on far less acquaintance in town; she had read of dukes marrying ladies they had only been introduced to a month before, after they had spent less than an hour together.

Some marriages were made, in the nobility, between people who had never met.

And being around Walter...it was as easy as breathing. Easier than anything Maria had known. Why, she had never felt this comfortable with even her own sisters.

Still...was it wrong? Something within her teased at her heart, whispering that she should not be considering talking to him.

What did she know about him really? Oh, all the important things: the way his eyes lit up when he smiled, the way he bit his thumb when thinking of something to say when he felt caught out...

But of his family, his nature...how could Maria be entirely sure of him?

"I hoped to see you," Maria found herself saying against all the instincts within her—instincts warring with her desires. She reached her hand in the bucket and scattered the feed to the geese, who honked in their eagerness. "I mean...I was unable to go for a walk today. I thought I would not see you."

"Yet here I am," said Walter with a grin. "On Chalcroft ground, though I do not suppose your father would begrudge me a look at the geese."

A flush tinged Maria's cheeks, and a strange prickle shot up her neck. Her father had not mentioned Walter since he had first come to the house, asking to see her mother—but then, why would he?

Her papa had no idea she had been seeing so much of Walter. The very idea of her father knowing the man he had so unceremoniously forced from his house had been kissing his daughter...

"What are you thinking about?"

Maria's whole body quivered at Walter's question. "Nothing."

She had spoken too quickly. A knowing look passed across his face, and he raised an eyebrow.

"Fine," said Maria. "You. There, are you happy?"

Walter stepped ever so slightly to the right, closer to her. "Very."

Was it possible to be this happy when not even touching?

Maria had never believed it possible, but she had not believed any gentleman would have noticed her in the midst of the Fitzroy clan.

Perhaps that was how she was able to attract Walter, she thought with a sinking feeling. He had only ever seen her alone.

Well, she would just have to keep it that way. Until…until what? Maria had tried thinking about the future, about what Walter could say to her, words that would make her so happy…so happy she would almost cry.

But she could not expect it. Walter was only here for a short time; he had mentioned that on one of their walks.

"Leaving so soon?" she had asked, hardly able to restrain herself.

And he had smiled and said, "Oh, not yet. I am not ready to go quite yet. Something…someone keeps me here."

And she had smiled and hoped beyond hope he meant her…

"Your geese seem happy."

Maria started, pulled from her reverie. She needed to concentrate or there was a very real chance she could slip and make a fool of herself. The snow on the ground had frozen into compact ice, and there was talk of more snow before Christmas Day. But the day was bright, her fingers not entirely chilled to the bone, and it was pleasant to stand here with the man she…a gentleman she greatly admired.

"Yes," said Maria with a laugh. "They are always happy when they are eating."

She placed her hand in the bucket once more and gasped as her fingers met those of another.

Walter. He had placed his hand into the bucket also and said nothing when their fingers touched—the first time their bare fingers had ever made contact.

Maria shivered, unable to move, only able to look at the man who had caused a sudden ripple of heat to shoot through her body. If that was what the mere contact of his fingers against hers could do…

"You always look after the geese?"

Maria shook her head. "No, not really. We have a woman for that, but I will admit I enjoy being with them. They seem to...well. They seem to feel sorrowful at this time of year."

Unsure why she was speaking so openly, Maria swallowed. It would be better if she ceased speaking altogether.

"Because the wild geese fly south."

Maria looked up. Walter was smiling gently, as though he had looked right into her mind and seen precisely what she had been thinking.

She nodded. "Instinct, I suppose. They fly south because they know they should be there, and I must admit I envy that at times."

"Instinct?"

"The...the knowledge that what one is doing is right," Maria confessed, hardly sure how she was able to this open. "I have never felt it. The instinct that one is in just the right place at the right time...with the right person."

Her eyes met his, fixed upon them. *As I am with you,* Maria wanted to say but could not bring herself to. *As I feel with you. As though this was meant to be, as though I am pulled towards you by something deep within me.*

"Geese never fly alone."

His voice was soft, searing into Maria's heart as she nodded. "No, they fly together. One leading at the front, all the others following them..."

"And none of them have ever laid golden eggs?" Walter spoke lightly, as though nothing had occurred.

Perhaps nothing had, Maria thought wildly. Perhaps she was too eager, getting ahead of herself, unable to prevent herself from thinking of scandalous fancies that were certainly not about to come true.

"G-Golden eggs?" she managed to repeat, removing her hand from the bucket and scattering feed across the pen.

Walter nodded, doing the same. "You know the old fairytale,

the goose that laid the golden eggs."

Maria laughed, her heart finally finding some equilibrium. "Yes, I know the story. Did the couple not become greedy, unwilling to wait for the daily egg, and kill the goose in order to get the gold from her insides?"

Walter joined her laughter. "And most sorry they must have been, too, when they realized their mistake. What a misfortune."

"Oh, I don't know," said Maria slowly, trying to prevent herself from moving closer to him. She could blame the cold, but that was not why she wished to be nearer. "Was it not their own greed that got them in the end? If they had just been patient, every day a glorious gift would have quite literally fallen into their laps."

Walter met her eyes. "And you have never found a golden egg nestled in the hay?"

Maria laughed. "No, sadly not. A golden egg or two certainly wouldn't go amiss in this household."

"Oh?"

Maria nodded, jerking her head back at Chalcroft, its elegant windows rising behind her. "It is a beautiful house, and I am very grateful live in it, of course, but still. You will not find a house more expensive to run than Chalcroft—at least, that is what my mother says."

"Really?" said Walter, taking a side step toward her.

Her heart pattered faster at the reduction of the gap between them of a few inches. She was in danger here, Maria knew, but could not bring herself to go inside.

Her heart was vulnerable, liable to get hurt if she was not careful. Just what were Walter's intentions toward her—and could they as wonderful as she hoped?

"Yes. I mean, it is quite a large house," said Maria, a little awkwardly. "But then in all our years of having geese, I have never found anything other than eggs. Imagine if we did!"

Walter smiled. "Imagine."

How did he do it, make her feel the center of the world when he looked at her?

Maria looked away from him for a moment and instead examined the geese, unable to hold such an intense gaze. It was impossible, whenever Walter looked at her like that, as though she was the most precious thing he had ever seen.

He had never said it, of course. Walter was rather reticent with his feelings. He did not need to speak his affections in words—she could feel them.

"It has not stopped my sister from telling the tale to her son, of course," Maria continued, a little breathless.

Oh, if only she was brave enough to close the gap between them, to kiss him, to put her arms around him and kiss him as she wanted to be kissed. To feel the dazzling heat of his body against hers, the strength of his arms around her, to know herself utterly at his mercy…

"Tale?"

"The goose who laid the golden eggs," said Maria, glancing at Walter with a wry smile.

It appeared she was not the only one to be slightly overwhelmed by the intensity of their unspoken feelings. Oh, if only he could say something—anything that would tell her just what he was thinking.

"I can imagine it was a tale well told," said Walter, moving so close to her now that Maria was unable to place her hand back in the bucket of feed. "I would like to hear it."

Maria blinked. It was a rather strange request, true, but there could be no harm in it. "Oh. Right. Well, the way my sister Olivia always starts it, there was once—"

"No, I meant, hear her tell the story," interrupted Walter with a winning smile on his face. "I would dearly love to hear it—perhaps I could come to dinner tonight. Or in a few days at Christmas. I assume one of these geese is for then?"

Maria swallowed, her heart skipping a beat most painfully.

I would dearly love to hear it—perhaps I could come to dinner tonight. Or in a few days, at Christmas. I assume one of these geese is for then?"

She had not felt as though she was doing anything wrong until that moment, until Walter requested an invitation to her father's table.

And, of course, she could not offer that. Not merely because it would be most uncouth of her to extend an invitation when it was her mother's place to do such a thing, but because she knew, did she not, precisely what her Papa would say at the thought of Walter appearing at his dinner table?

"Well, if he comes to the front door again, you are not to let him in, you understand?"

Maria had not questioned it, not asked her father why Walter was not to be permitted entrance to the house. He had not heard her father's words, could not know she was forbidden from bringing him inside—not that she had heeded the spirit of the order, meeting him so frequently outside.

She swallowed, tasting fear in her throat. She was rebelling in a way she had never expected, standing here with Walter, talking with him, kissing him.

And she knew so little about him: where he came from, his family, why he was here, in the West Country in the first place.

"Maria?"

"I…I do not think that will be possible," Maria said weakly.

"Oh?" Walter moved his hand to hers, gently removing the bucket of feed from her fingers and placing it on the ground. Then he took her hands in his own. "And why not?"

Maria hesitated, looking up into his eyes. There was such innocence there, such eagerness. Yet at the same time, something else. Something Walter was holding back. Something she did not understand, and he had never shared.

Which was within his right, of course. She could not expect him to share everything with her, not immediately.

But with her father's warning ringing in her ears, Maria knew she could not do it. Walter had to be her secret, and hers alone— at least for the present. Later, when she knew him better, could perhaps fathom precisely what misunderstanding her father had about him—for it must be a misunderstanding; no one who knew Walter could possibly dislike him—she could bring together the two men she loved most in the world and make them understand not only how much she cared for each of them, but how they should respect each other.

But not yet. That would take time.

Forcing a bright smile upon her face, Maria shrugged as though nothing important at all had just rushed through her mind.

"No particular reason," she said lightly. "'Tis just…well, you know. Christmas is a time for family, and my family are spending it together this year."

Walter nodded, stroking her fingers with his own. Maria's breath caught in her throat, such longing, such desire was racing through her she could barely think to breathe.

Oh, she wanted him to touch far more than her hands. In a flash, she imagined those fingers gently stroking her face, her collarbone, his fingers brushing against her breasts—

"Quite understandable," said Walter cheerfully, forcing Maria from her reverie. "Now, why don't you show me around this delightful farm of yours?"

CHAPTER FIVE

T HE BELLS OF Chalcroft church rang out into the frosty air as the Fitzroy family spilled out of the front porch.

"Wonderful service," Maria's Papa said warmly to the vicar who looked a little startled to be spoken to by the head of the Fitzroy family. "Really enjoyable."

"It is not supposed to be enjoyable, it is supposed to make you think," murmured Olivia primly, while Kitty made a face behind her back, making Tommy snort with laughter.

Maria smiled as she watched them. More of the villagers were now coming out of the church and conversing with each other, catching up with neighbors, sharing pleasant gossip, looking at everyone in their fine Sunday best.

There was something about living in a small village—at least, just outside one. Gossip was everywhere, yes, but much of it was well-meaning. The latest fashions that Miss So-and-So had ordered from Bath, the way that Mr. You-Know looked at his sister's best friend at the last country dance…

"—and I said, it cannot be true, I know Mrs. Fitzroy myself, and there was never a kinder nor a more generous woman in all of England!"

Maria's smile faltered. That dratted newspaper article. She had not given it much thought after her father had read it aloud, but she had noticed a strange sort of gloom over her mother since its publication, and it appeared they were not the only people who had read it.

Clearly there were more readers of that paper, whatever it was, than she had thought. Readers who had clearly believed the gossiping slander about her mother were shooting the Fitzroy family strange looks—looks she did not like.

For the speaker she had overheard was right. Her mother was generous, sometimes to a fault. The amount of time she spent on those Christmas presents—and the Easter presents! No maid ever left the Fitzroy family without a substantial dowry if she chose to be married, and no footman had ever gone without a reference if he wished to take a position elsewhere.

The idea that anyone could believe such terrible things about her mother…her father was right, it was an outrage!

"A newcomer," said Isabella, nudging her.

Maria blinked, forced out of her thoughts. "What?"

Her sister nodded in the direction of the vicarage cottage, which had been left empty for so long. "There. A newcomer, a stranger to Chalcroft."

Maria looked, intrigued, and joy swelled in her heart as the sight of Walter Arborn appeared before her. Dressed in a remarkably fashionable coat and top hat, he was walking toward the cottage he had taken for the festive season.

"Have you ever seen such a top hat?" Isabella wondered aloud. "The ribbon alone must have cost…I have never—Maria?"

Maria did not respond to her sister. She was already too far away, her feet taking her down the path around the church, toward Walter's cottage.

She had to be close to him. She had to follow him, it was not a decision she made but rather a pull from just under her navel, one she could not ignore, even if she had wanted to. And she did not want to.

Ever since their conversation at the goose pen yesterday, Maria had been unable to get the young man out of her mind. He was…special. There was something about him, something far more than mere attractiveness, though there was plenty of that, too.

He was someone she cared for. Maria could not explain it, had no desire to examine it, just wanting to feel it, to lose herself in it.

Walter was a little way ahead on her on the path and did not seem to have noticed her, and Maria was overcome with the instinct to call out after him.

But something within her hesitated. Her entire family was behind her, likely as not watching her in bemusement, unsure as to why she chasing after a gentleman they had never seen—other than her father.

A strange shiver of cold rushed through Maria. *Except her father.* He had already forbidden the man from the house, and that was before knowing anything about him. It was a strange preoccupation, now she came to think of it. Most unlike her father to take against someone without at least having a reason to do so.

But Walter was gaining on her, pulling farther away, and the terrible thought that he may enter the cottage and force her to knock.

"Walter!"

Her cry was soft but urgent, and it did its work. The gentleman halted, turned, and smiled at the woman who was following him.

"You know," he said pleasantly as Maria caught up with him, just around the corner of the cottage and away from any prying eyes outside the church, "I think that is the first time you have called me 'Walter' without me asking you to."

Heat flushed Maria's cheeks, and she looked at the ground before lifting her gaze. "Perhaps."

Walter smiled, a winning smile that made Maria quiver to the very depths of her toes. Was she a fool to feel this way? Did everyone feel this overwhelmed, this foolish, this marvelous when they came across a certain someone?

Or was she the only fool in existence?

"Yes?" Walter prompted.

Maria blinked. "Yes?"

He laughed. "Well, you were the one who called out to me, Maria, and though I am glad of it, I wondered if there was a particular reason that you did so."

"Oh!" Maria smiled awkwardly, wishing she had a purpose for accosting him.

All I want to do is be with you, she wanted to say. *And I do not understand it, and a part of me does not need it explained. Just being with you is enough.*

"Nothing...nothing in particular," she said lamely.

Oh, if only she had the rapidity of tongue of her sisters—any of them!

"*Instinct, I suppose. They fly south because they know they should be there, and I must admit I envy that at times.*"

"Instinct?"

"*The...the knowledge that what one is doing is right. I have never felt it. The instinct that one is in just the right place, at the right time...with the right person.*"

Maria swallowed. If she was going to make her own match— and she knew she was a fool to even think that she would be able to convince Walter to see her more than someone worth kissing—then she would have to say something. Anything. *Anything!*

"I...I wanted to speak to you," she said, hearing the anxiety in her voice.

Walter raised an eyebrow. "About...?"

Maria took a deep breath and knew there was no going back now. "About anything. About you. About...about whatever you wish to speak on."

She looked up at him, hoping Walter could see in her eyes what was in her heart: that any conversation with him was worth far more than the niceties and politeness of normal Society.

And perhaps he did. A slow smile of understanding crept

across his face as he extended his arm.

"Miss Fitzroy, would you do me the pleasure of accompanying me on a short walk in the woodlands behind my cottage?"

Maria almost laughed, the pretend pomposity was so ridiculous—but she played along, heart pattering, unsure where this was going to go but knowing that she wanted it, whatever it was, more than anything.

"Why, yes, Mr. Arborn," she said haughtily, "I will."

She placed her arm in his, felt the shiver of pleasure she always did when she was close to him, so close she could breathe him in, and they started to walk slowly along the path.

Speed was not important. Maria did not want to walk quickly anyway; she wanted to walk as slowly as she could, enjoy every moment, take it all in, remember it forever.

Who knew if she would ever have such an experience again? Why, it was almost like courting.

"I was pleased to see your family in church today," Walter said conversationally, all hauteur gone.

Maria breathed a laugh. "Yes, all of us, and we seem to grow in number every year! My smallest nephew, Fred, is but a few months old."

"How pleasant for your parents to see their family grow."

Maria considered this for a moment. She supposed it was, although it certainly brought an increase in noise and mess whenever Olivia, Kitty, and their families returned to Chalcroft. She would not change it for anything though, despite the ruckus to her life, and she was almost sure her parents felt the same.

"Yes, it is lovely," she said as they meandered around a corner, the woodlands seemingly deserted other than a few birds in the trees. "I know my mother in particular adores having everyone back. She has no other family, you see."

"Really?" came the swift question from Walter. "Truly, no other family?"

Maria shook her head. "Papa has two brothers, and I see my Fitzroy cousins regularly. Why, we heard from Lucy only a few days ago, one of my cousins who lives in London, and she said—"

"No siblings whatsoever?" interrupted Walter, his gaze on her, fiercely interested in a way she had never seen before. "No family in Italy she has spoken of, no relatives who have ever come to Chalcroft to visit you?"

Maria opened her mouth, hesitated, then closed it again. For the first time since she had met Walter, and it felt like an age ago, a prickle of discomfort in his presence arched its way up her back.

There it was again—a pointed question about her mother, one he would not let lie when she answered it in a haphazard way and moved onto another topic.

"No siblings whatsoever? No family in Italy that she has spoken of, no relatives who have ever come to Chalcroft to visit you?"

As it happened, Maria was not aware of any family in Italy. Her mother had certainly never spoken of any and none had come to England, let alone Chalcroft, claiming them.

But that was beside the point. Why was Walter so interested in her mother? Where were all these questions leading?

"I…I do not know," Maria lied softly.

Walter halted, turning to look at her as he disentangled his arm from hers. "You are lying."

Maria blanched. There was no anger in his voice, no disappointment, just a calm statement of fact. "You cannot possibly know that."

"I know you," said Walter softly. "Better than you could know, Maria. I bet…I bet I can make you tell me."

The way he was looking at her…Maria knew she should feel afraid, perhaps, or at the very least suspicious of this man who seemed to want nothing but to kiss her and find out details about her family, for whatever reason.

But the way he had spoken—excitement flickered across her body at the very thought of him making her do anything.

"I bet you cannot," Maria whispered, not taking her eyes from him.

The woods were silent. Even the birds were silent, for all

Maria could hear. The only sound was her heart, racing in her chest and making her pulse throb in her ears.

A wicked smile curled the corners of Walter's lips. "Well, it is a bet then. Come on."

He strode over to a large oak tree, a few feet from the path, and stood before it expectantly. Maria followed him, curiosity overcoming her better judgment. Just how did he think an oak tree would make her say anything?

"Stand there, with your back to the tree," said Walter quietly. "And remove your pelisse."

Maria's fingers leapt protectively to the fastenings of her pelisse. "Why? I'll be cold."

There was that wicked smile again, but it was not unpleasant. Quite to the contrary, Maria found to her surprise it made Walter all the more devilishly handsome.

"You will not be cold," he murmured, not taking his eyes from her. "I promise you."

Unsure precisely why she was obeying, but finding herself unable to prevent herself, Maria's fingers fumbled at the fastenings of her pelisse and let it fall to the ground without looking away from Walter's eyes. She took a step back and felt the rough bark against her back.

"Good," said Walter, taking a step toward her.

He was so close, for a moment Maria was certain he was going to kiss her, and she arched her back to reach his lips—but just at the last moment, he pulled away.

"And now," he said softly, "close your eyes."

"No," said Maria instinctively.

Whatever this was, whatever game he was playing, it was too much. Maria could feel her whole body tingling, desperate for whatever Walter was going to do, but at the same time she held back.

This was dangerous. This was delicious. This was more than she could ever have imagined, and it was happening right now, to her.

Walter examined her for a moment, then jerked his head as though it did not matter to him. "Fine. Now, here are the rules of the game. Every time I get an answer I like, you'll get this."

He closed the gap, capturing his lips with hers, and Maria lost herself in the kiss, wild and passionate and deep—and then she gasped in his mouth.

While his lips were ravaging hers, Walter's hands had not been idle. One of them had moved to cover her secret place, a finger teasingly stroked across it, causing sharp jolts of pleasure to rocket through her.

"I-I like that," Maria managed to gasp, barely able to see, the intensity of that moment had been so overwhelming.

Now she knew why Walter had told her to close her eyes.

"I know you like it," murmured Walter, his eyes fixed on hers and a smile of delight on his face. "And I like giving it to you, Maria, but only if I get answers I like. It's a game."

Maria's breath was tight in her chest, and she wanted to moan for more of the pleasure just one of his fingers was able to give her.

"I know you. Better than you could know, Maria. I bet...I bet I can make you tell me."

She had underestimated him, Maria knew, and now as her body craved the touch it had only just experienced, she knew he had complete power over her.

Not looking away, knowing Walter was watching her closely, Maria placed her hands on the tree trunk on either side of her, and slowly, ever so slowly, closed her eyes. Darkness fell. Darkness that promised so much.

She heard Walter groan. "God, you are so...Maria, I have wanted to do this for a long time."

And his lips crushed hers, and Maria gave herself up to the kiss, restraining her hands from reaching out to grasp him, to pull him closer, and she moaned with disappointment as the kiss ended, his fingers absent from her secret place that now throbbed for him.

"And now we begin the game," came Walter's voice, and Maria quivered in anticipation. "Do you enjoy Christmas, Maria?"

"Enjoy—enjoy Christmas?" In darkness, Maria could not understand why Walter had asked her that. *What had that got to do with her mother?*

"Answer the question, Maria." Walter's voice was dark and dangerous and close, and Maria ached to have him touch her again.

"Yes," she breathed. "Oh!"

Walter's fingers had moved back to her secret place, clutching between her legs, and the stroke was strong, she could feel every iota of movement through her gown. Maria quivered at the sensation of it, pleasure sparking across her legs.

"Do your sisters enjoy Christmas?"

"Yes," Maria breathed, and was immediately rewarded by another stroke—sensuous and deep but gone too soon. "Ask me more, ask me more!"

A chuckle from Walter, but Maria did not care. She just wanted the strokes to go on and on, building towards something she did not understand, but knew she wanted.

"Are your sisters happy with their husbands?"

"Yes," Maria whimpered, anticipation overwhelming her as Walter's strokes this time continued, giving her more than one, and her back arched against the tree, the pleasure making it difficult to stay still, and anyone could come upon them at any moment but that did not matter. "Yes, yes, yes…"

"What about your other sister?"

"Isabella?" Maria felt his hand disappear, knew she was being punished. "She—she is lonely I think, I am not much company. Oh, Walter!"

She could not help it. Maria quivered, desperate for more pleasure as his fingers returned to her. This time, Walter cleverly twisted the fabric of her gown, and it was as though his finger was inside her. Of course, it was not, the soft muslin provided a barrier, but Maria was seeing stars, eyes still closed, at the intensity of the pleasure.

"Maria," came Walter's voice, a whisper, right by her ear, and Maria moaned to feel him so close, "have you been good this Christmas?"

"Yes," Maria whimpered.

In an instant, his hand was removed, and Maria stood there in darkness in bewilderment, not understanding what had happened—until…

"No," Maria breathed. "No, I have not been good."

Walter's mouth crushed hers, and his fingers were inside her, somehow, through her gown, Maria did not know how, but she could feel him, and he was stroking her, teasing her, and heat was building and building, pleasure she had never felt before reaching her very toes. Maria cried out in his mouth as her whole body exploded, the tree and Walter's hands the only thing keeping her upright.

As the pleasure faded, slowly retreating like a tide on a beach, Maria slowly opened her eyes, hazy with pleasure, to see Walter right before her.

"Oh, Maria," he murmured, kissing her neck as his hands remained on her hips, holding her upright. "That was…"

"I do not know what that was," said Maria in a jagged voice, still conscious that anyone could come along the path and find them, "but I want more of it."

Walter laughed, a rough laugh that suggested he had been similarly affected, though Maria could not understand how—just as she could not quite understand what had just happened to her, that was not surprising.

"Dear God, Maria, I never had you pegged for…Christ, I would like to do that to you again."

Maria removed a hand from the tree trunk to gently grasp his chin, lifting Walter's eyes to her own. "You would?"

Walter nodded slowly, not looking away from her.

Letting out a breath slowly, Maria tried to think. She should not be doing this. This was the sort of thing scandalous harlots did—though now she had a taste, she understood why.

Who would not want to do such things?

"But I should not," said Walter quietly with a knowing smile across his face. "Should I?"

Maria hesitated, but only for a moment. *Now the line was crossed, what did it matter?*

"No," she said with a nervous smile, removing her hand from his chin and instead capturing his fingers in hers, moving them down to her secret place and gasping at the prickles of pleasure already building up at the mere anticipation of such wicked decadence. "No, we really shouldn't."

CHAPTER SIX

"—TIDINGS OF COMFORT and joy, comfort and joy…"

Maria sang along with her family, all the Fitzroys gathered around the pianoforte—except for Fred, who was asleep upstairs, and Tommy. He appeared to be on an expedition to clamber over the sofa, but Olivia was keeping an eye on him, so Maria did nothing to prevent him.

"—tidings of comfort and joy!"

Gentle applause rang out at the end of the carol, and Maria's Papa put a congratulatory hand on Isabella's shoulder.

"Very good, my dear, very good. I only counted six wrong notes."

He ducked away from the teasing slap of his daughter's hand, and Maria laughed with the rest of the family. This was what Christmas had always been with the Fitzroys, whether they invited the Bath or London branches of the family, or whether they invited friends and neighbors as they did a few years ago, when Olivia and Luke had discovered their feelings for each other.

Music, laughter, food. So much food. Maria glanced at the tray of mince pies. She had already indulged in two, the sticky sweetness of the pastry cloying to the palate.

Maria sighed happily. This Christmas was shaping up to be everything that she wanted—and a few things she had not realized, before this week, that she had wanted as well.

"I know you. Better than you could know, Maria. I bet…I bet I can make you tell me."

She shivered, hoping none of her family had noticed the sudden heat flaring in her cheeks.

It was starting to become a recurring problem, whenever she allowed her mind to wander back to Walter. To the way he touched her, the way he kissed her. The things he could do with his fingers…

Maria had not even known it was possible to do such things, feel such things. Knowing now what she did, it was painful to stand here with her family around the pianoforte, singing Christmas carols after dinner.

Not when she knew precisely where she wanted to be…

The image of the cottage just outside the vicarage where Walter would, right now, be spending the evening alone popped into Maria's mind, and she did not push it away.

The temptation to just leave her family to their singing to find Walter first occurred to her when Isabella had suggested they sing together, and it had only been growing ever since.

It was a scandalous idea, one Maria would never have considered before today. But the idea of being with Walter was a heady one, one that twisted her heart and made her sure it was far more exciting than this dull evening.

"Which shall we sing next?" asked Olivia, rifling through the stacks of paper. "Isabella, did you write this one out by hand?"

"Well, I could not find the sheet music, and I thought it far better to be written out poorly by me than not have it at all," said Isabella reasonably. "Careful, Tommy!"

The entire family looked around. Tommy had managed to tip himself upside down, legs on the sofa and head on the floor, giggling away to himself at the predicament he had found himself in.

"Oh, Tommy!" Olivia rushed toward her son, almost audibly clucking with concern, while her husband roared with laughter.

"It's not funny, Luke!"

"It absolutely is," said Isaac fairly. "Little chap doesn't seem concerned, does he?"

The Fitzroys watched Olivia "rescue" her son from the strange position he had found himself in, but Maria was not unduly concerned. Her nephew was roaring with laughter at all the attention he was receiving, which was all to the good, and his distraction provided her with the perfect excuse.

After all, it was not as though she had orchestrated this opportunity. It had just…happened. And it would be foolish of her not to use it to her advantage.

Holding her breath, as though that would make any sort of difference, Maria crept toward the door to the hall. She stepped softly, her eyes fixed on her family, but none of them looked around to see where she was going.

No surprises there, Maria thought with a smile as she gently closed the drawing room door behind her. She was the quiet one, after all, the one who avoided as much attention as possible. They were accustomed to her not being in the room with them.

What they did not know was that very soon, she would not even be in the house.

Slipping on her pelisse and trying not to think of the last time she had taken it off, falling to the woodland floor just before Walter…

Maria swallowed. She had crossed a line no young lady with any hope of maintaining her reputation should cross, yet her heart soared at the thought of seeing Walter again.

What had he done to her?

The night air was freezing as she slipped out of the side door and crept around the house. Chalcroft looked magnificent in the festive moonlight, and Maria saw her breath blossom out before her as she hurried on her way.

The church was not that far away—perhaps a fifteen-minute walk? And the cottage right beside it, and within it…Walter.

Maria's footsteps hastened, heart thumping so loudly that

when an owl swooped past her, she jolted.

What was she doing?

Maria hardly knew herself. She did not know what she wanted to happen when she knocked on Walter's door and saw him standing there. Would she ask to be invited in? Would she perhaps…stay the night with him?

She was hardly an innocent—certainly not now—and Maria knew there was far more a gentleman and a lady could explore together. She had never known, never realized just how much pleasure could be accompanied by such things, but now she knew…

Well. It was tempting.

Maria swallowed down her fear as the church steeple came into view. What she was doing…what she was considering was far more rebellious than anything she had ever thought of before, but it did not seem possible to turn back.

Maria's heart stirred as she saw the cottage ahead of her, a little light escaping the curtains in the window. He understood her better than anyone, better than herself. He saw something in her, Maria was sure, no one else had ever seen. Something she did not see herself.

She loved him. Maria may not have put it in words, not yet; she could barely put the thoughts together, in truth.

But what else could this be? What else felt like this, this overwhelming sensation that they had to be together? That nothing else in the world mattered as long as she was with him?

That even standing up to her father and telling him she had fallen in love with a man he had forbidden from the house was worth it if she could be Walter's wife?

Walter's wife.

Maria forced the thoughts away as she stepped onto the path leading up to the cottage door. She needed to put all those foolish thoughts from her mind. Walter was not about to propose matrimony to her. Not yet, at least.

Bravery she had never felt before soared through her veins,

and Maria smiled as she reached the front door, its charming rustic knocker just before her.

Well, she had done it. Something a few years ago—few months ago, few weeks ago!—she would never have considered. She had secretly left home, leaving her parents and sisters behind, all to meet a gentleman who did not even know she was coming. It felt strange, yes, but it felt right. As the wintery wind blew past her, Maria tugging her pelisse closer, she knew. This was where she was supposed to be.

All she wanted was for Walter to touch her again...

Spurred on by the thought, Maria reached out a hand and knocked gently on the door. Really all she did was lift the knocker and allow it to fall.

She waited. He may be finishing his dinner or reading a book. Perhaps he did not hear the knocker; perhaps she had been too delicate with it.

Heart racing, hardly knowing what she was doing, Maria lifted the knocker, and this time rapped hard on the door, not once, not twice, but three times.

Maria waited. And waited. Eventually, thought she did not like the conclusion, she had to accept the truth. Walter was not there.

Disappointment such as she had never known almost overpowered her, and Maria leaned against the door. *He was not here.* Surely if he had heard the door, he would have come to open it—which meant he was elsewhere. Where? Walter had not mentioned any invitations. To the contrary, he had emphasized whenever asking for an invitation to Chalcroft that he was very much alone in these parts.

All the tension, which had built in her shoulders, seeped away, and Maria hung her head. After all her bravery, her cleverness to use her nephew as a diversion, it did not matter.

Walter was not here.

Although it had taken her but fifteen minutes to reach the cottage from her home, it felt like a lifetime trudging back. Every step felt heavier, the distance farther, the wind up so high she had to lean into it to keep going.

By the time Maria had reached the side door she felt exhausted, all hope of a pleasant evening scuppered. She would have to return to the drawing room, give some sort of explanation as to why she had been absent for the last half an hour or so, and then likely as not, join in with more carols.

She could only hope that Kitty would be playing the pianoforte by now.

Just as Maria lifted her hand to open the side door, a voice spoke from the darkness.

"Maria."

She turned quickly toward the voice. There he was, coming out from behind a tree.

A slow smile crept across her face as her heart settled with joy at the sight of him. "What are you doing out here at this time?"

Walter did not appear to be concerned at her tone. "Hoping for a chance to see you, of course."

Happiness flooded through Maria's heart. Of course he was. He could no more stay away from her than she could from him. They were so connected, even across a distance, that as she had been creeping to his house to see him, Walter had been doing the same.

"What a shame we missed each other," Maria said lightly, wondering whether he could see in the dull gloom of the night just how thrilled she was to see him. "I have just been to your cottage. I was certain you were there, the light was on."

"Oh, I leave a candle lit so I always have light to return home to," said Walter with a shrug of his shoulders, stepping toward her. "It makes it less lonely."

Maria leaned against the wall of the house as he approached her, her gaze catching his, and she poured into it all the longing she felt, longing she could not describe in words.

And he understood, of course he did. Instead of halting a few feet from her, as would have been polite, Walter kept going—

kept walking forward until he was right before her, his hands taking hers, his lips kissing hers so passionately that Maria's head spun.

He wanted her; she wanted him. They were equals in that, even if he was handsome and charming and came from London and seen so much more of the world than she had.

Maria's fingers entangled themselves in Walter's hair, pulling him close, and he responded in kind, his hands moving to her buttocks and drawing her close—so close she could feel the hardness of him as she gasped in his mouth.

"Maria…" Walter broke the kiss and looked deep into her eyes, but he did not seem able to go on.

Maria smiled encouragingly, heart racing, wondering what he wished to say.

She watched him swallow, his gaze dropping, then lifting again to meet hers, as though he was determined to say something. She saw the fear in him, the terror his words may not be met with the same sentiments.

And she knew then, as she had never known before, precisely what Walter wanted to say.

He wished to declare his love for her.

It was so obvious, painted across his face. Maria's heart leapt, every part of her quivering, as she knew herself to be loved just as much as she loved him.

It was a miracle—but the worst of it was, Walter did not appear to know where to begin.

"Maria, I—there is something I must tell you," Walter said all in a rush, and Maria smiled, hoping to encourage him wordlessly. "I…oh, damn, it is impossible to know where to begin. Maria, I—"

"I love you, too," said Maria impetuously.

She had not been able to help it. Watching him struggle to find the words, not quite sure how to say what was on his heart, unsure how his words would be received…it was an experience she knew all too well and she could not permit him to struggle with it alone.

Walter gaped at her, his hands still on her buttocks. "Y-You…you do?"

Maria nodded, sliding her hands to his neck and beaming up at him. Finally, they understood each other. Finally, all boundaries between them had been removed. The instincts that had drawn them together, as the geese flew south, finally resolved. Finally, this Christmas, she would be the Fitzroy sister who had found her true love.

"Yes," she said, hardly knowing where this boldness was coming from. A wellspring of affection in the deepest depths of her heart that she hardly knew she had had revealed itself. "Oh, Walter, I have never met anyone like you—anyone who makes me feel what you make me feel."

He chuckled wryly at that. "I should think not!"

Maria laughed, flushing at his words. "Not like that—well, like that, but also…oh, Walter. You talk to me as though…as though I am interesting in my own right."

"But you are!"

"You would be surprised," said Maria, trying to keep bitterness from her voice. "Being a Fitzroy…there are certain expectations that come with being a part of my family, and I have never…but when I am with you…"

Walter smiled, his joy radiating from his face, visible even in the darkness of the night. "You truly are something quite special, you know that, Maria?"

Maria swallowed. She did not know that. Hearing it aloud, for the first time—from the lips of the man she loved…it was something she had never expected to feel or know. And it was happening. This was not a dream.

Lifting up her face once again to be kissed, Walter lowered his head but just halted a mere half an inch from her mouth. Maria moaned, desperate for the connection, and tried to reach him, moving onto her tip toes, but Walter kept himself just out of reach.

A desire, a need Maria was only now starting to understand

was building up within her, deep within, between her legs, and she moaned again at the desperate need.

"Walter—"

"Isn't it fun?" he whispered, his hands tight on her buttocks. "Just to tease you, just a little…"

Then he kissed her, his tongue teasing her own as pleasure rippled through Maria's body, the final kiss far more intense than she could have imagined.

"Walter," Maria said hurriedly, breaking the kiss and looking up at the man she loved. "Come upstairs with me."

For a moment, Walter frowned, obviously not understand. "Come…come upstairs?"

Maria nodded, her tongue suddenly mute as the impact of what she had said started to unfurl in her heart.

"Walter. Come upstairs with me."

Well, it was an invitation she should never have made, but it came from a place deep within her; a knowledge that before long, they would be man and wife, so what did it matter, really? It was just a case of dates, that was all. Whether the wedding happened before or after Walter bedded her…did it make much of a difference?

Maria saw the spark of desire in his eyes as understanding flooded through him, and she shivered with anticipation. He wanted her. She knew it, knew it as viscerally as she knew she wanted him. Aching for his touch was only fun for so long.

Now she needed him to satisfy that ache.

"Upstairs?" he repeated with a mischievous grin. "Without your family knowing, I take it?"

Maria swallowed as the memory of her father's words overtook her.

"Well, if he comes to the front door again, you are not to let him in, you understand?"

But her Papa had said the front door, Maria reasoned, desperate desire overtaking her thinking. He said nothing about the side door—and really, once her father got to know Walter, it would be a completely different conversation.

"Without anyone knowing, yes," Maria breathed, removing her hands from Walter's neck and taking his hands in hers. "Come on. Do you…do you want to?"

For a heady moment, Maria thought Walter may actually decline her invitation. There may be something of the gentleman in him that prevented him from it, she worried, and all this aching and desire would be for nothing.

Then a wicked grin crept across Walter's face. "Shall we?"

CHAPTER SEVEN

MARIA COULD HARDLY believe it—could still hear her own words echoing in her mind, as though she was saying them over and over again.

"Without anyone knowing, yes. Come on. Do you…do you want to?"

What did she think she was doing? Inviting a gentleman up to her bedchamber—a gentleman, no less, who had already kissed her most profusely, whom she had only met but a few weeks ago?

"I…oh, damn, it is impossible to know where to begin. Maria, I—"

"I love you, too."

But what did that matter? As Maria looked up into his eyes, saw the desire in them, saw how Walter looked at her…she knew.

Beyond a shadow of a doubt.

Walter cared for her, cared far more than she had expected. A gentleman like him—handsome, charming—had never been what she had expected, yet here she was, ready to share with him something that only married people did.

What did she think she was doing, risking her reputation like this—for a gentleman? No title, no riches, no wealth that she was aware of, no particular note of any kind?

Maria looked at Walter, and her heart skipped a beat.

None of that mattered. She had not been like Olivia, determined to marry well. She was not even like Kitty, demanding that any gentleman who expected to win her heart had to work hard at impressing her.

No, Maria was always in the background of her own life it seemed, but now, finally, someone saw her for what she was. Someone worthy.

She swallowed, trying to take in the last few minutes, though it was a challenge. What Fitzroy would ever do something so scandalous?

A memory surfaced from a few years ago: the family outside Chalcroft, staring at Kitty who had been discovered most unusually coming out of a barn in the early hours of the morning with a man who would turn out, eventually, to become her husband.

Perhaps she was not the first Fitzroy to ever do such a thing, then, but still. Kitty was far more opinionated, far more sure of herself.

This was not something Olivia nor Isabella would ever have dreamed of.

But it was happening.

"Ready?" whispered Walter, as though he was worried they would be overheard.

Maria nodded. They certainly would not be overheard as long as they were careful, and she saw no reason for anyone to discover them.

She was decided on this course, no regret peeping into her heart to slow her down. This was what she wanted. Who she wanted. In the darkness of the night, when the rest of the world faded from view, all she could see was him. All she wanted was him.

"I...I am ready," Maria breathed, hardly understanding how she could speak. "Come with me."

When her questing fingers were finally able to find his own, Maria found to her surprise that Walter's pulse appeared to be faster than her own, which was rocketing through her body at great speed.

Perhaps he was as nervous, as excited, as unsure as she was.

Heartened by this thought, Maria's free hand reached for the side door handle. The creak of the door hinges cracked into the night. Only darkness lay within, but her eyes had grown accustomed to the darkness during her passionate kissing with the gentleman who followed her silently into the corridor.

Maria closed the door behind them. It slid shut with a gentle thump.

There. The first barrier had been overcome. Walter was inside the house.

She had expected to feel a strange rebellion in her chest, but all Maria could sense was delight at the idea of what was to come next. Of what they would share.

"This way," she breathed.

The two of them stepped lightly along the corridor, joy trapped in Maria's heart. At every moment she expected a servant to appear, perhaps a housemaid dampening down the fires, or a footman sent to polish something in advance of Christmas.

But they met not a soul.

It was fortunate, indeed, Maria knew the back corridors so well. The girls had played there as children and still used them on occasion to avoid their mother when she was in a particularly foul temper, so she needed neither light nor candle to find her way.

Before Maria could believe it was possible, her fingers were closing on the door handle to her very own bedchamber.

A creak. A floorboard squeaked slightly under their footsteps and Maria froze, glancing to the doors on either side of her own. One was empty, an unused guest room. One held Isabella.

Walter followed her lead, staying absolutely still as they stood there in the silence, waiting for an indication someone had heard them.

But all was quiet.

Maria let out a slow breath, hardly aware she had been hold-ing it so long, and knew she had to make absolutely sure. It would not do for them to be…well. Interrupted.

Heart thundering in her chest, she let go of Walter's hand and stepped towards her sister's bedchamber.

"Maria!"

She ignored Walter's warning, just waving a hand behind her to keep him quiet, and carefully opened the door.

The room was empty.

Maria smiled weakly as she turned back to Walter, waiting hesitantly in the corridor. "'Tis quite all right—my sister sometimes sleeps in another room if her headache ails her. The breeze is different, she always says. She's at the other end of the house."

A look of deep relief overcame Walter's expression. "So…so we are alone?"

"On this corridor, yes," whispered Maria, not entirely sure why she was whispering as there was no one to hear them. "We are quite alone."

Quite alone. It was a strange thought. Maria had so rarely been alone with a gentleman; in fact, now she came to think of it, Walter was the only man she had ever been truly alone with.

And now…

Maria gently turned the handle of the door to her bedchamber.

Light spilled out into the corridor. The candle that was always placed on her bedside table by a servant was still alit, gifting a gentle glow to the room and now to the corridor beyond. Like a beacon, it drew them closer, and Maria leaned against her door as she closed it, looking into her bedchamber which now suddenly felt half its size.

Was that normal, when a gentleman entered a bedchamber?

Pulse throbbing in her ears, senses heightened, and still half certain someone would hear them, Maria looked at Walter as he took in his surroundings.

He was such a handsome man. Taller than she had realized, now he was standing in the middle of her bedchamber.

He turned to her. "Right. Well."

Maria's stomach dropped. The hesitancy in his voice was marked, unable to be ignored. He had made no move to approach her, no attempt to close the gap between them.

It was intolerable.

She could see it now; he had changed his mind. Despite their passionate kissing downstairs, Walter did not actually wish to…Maria hardly knew what the words were for it.

Make love to her?

He did not really want her. Perhaps he was just using her, a form of entertainment while he was here in the sleepy countryside. Perhaps he had not expected her to go through with her offer.

Maria's shoulders slumped. *She should have guessed.* She should have known a gentleman as handsome as him did not really desire her.

Well, she would have to make it clear he could leave. Even if her heart was breaking. Even if she could bear to look at him.

"You do not have to—"

"I want you to be sure—"

Maria looked up. At the precise moment she had attempted to let Walter know she bore him no ill will for wishing to change his mind, Walter, too, had spoken—yet his words did not make sense.

He wanted her to be sure? She had invited him into her bedchamber, had she not? How much more sure did he think she could be?

"I beg your pardon?" she breathed, her gaze flickering across his features.

Walter smiled ruefully. "I just…damnit, Maria, if I had my way, you would already be on that bed there."

Heat seared Maria's cheeks, but she did not look away. It was intoxicating, hearing these words from Walter. As though he truly cared for her. As though he could do nothing but long for her.

"But I want you to be sure—really sure—that this is what you want," Walter continued in a low voice, his gaze not leaving hers. "There is no way back from this, Maria, once we have shared this. And I want to, but…you have to be sure."

Maria swallowed. *No way back.* Well, he was right about that—only he was wrong about when that turning point occurred. It was already too late for her. She loved him. Knew it, even if she could not quite articulate it yet.

There would never be another man for her.

"You…you are…" Maria licked her lips and saw with startled pleasure what a reaction that gained from Walter. "You are…the goose."

Walter blinked. "I beg your pardon?"

Maria almost laughed. *How could he not see?* "You are my goose, the goose that laid the golden egg. The goose that flew west to me…oh Walter, you have showed me pleasure, showed me what it is to be…to be kissed, to be held, to be loved. And I want more."

Confusion disappeared from Walter's eyes, and he stepped forward, lust sparking across his face. "Yes?"

Maria nodded. "I…I want you to be the only person who ever kisses me. Touches me like—like that. Loves me like that."

He was standing right before her now, out of reach. Tempting as it was to pull him toward her, Maria just about managed to resist. Just.

"Well, in that case," said Walter in a low voice, reaching to take her hand in his. "I am afraid you will have to answer a few more questions."

Maria shivered, the memory of that wonderful moment against the tree surfacing in her mind. Oh, if he was going to do such things to her…she was not sure whether she could bear it.

Yet she knew she would.

"So, Maria Fitzroy," Walter said softly as he pulled her to the center of the room. "What is your full name?"

"Maria Leonora Fitzroy," breathed Maria as his fingers

wound their way in her hair, removing her hairpins.

Within a moment, her long dark hair had fallen to her shoulders. It was all too much. Maria could hardly bear it. This was far more intimate than she had ever been with any other gentleman.

Just what could come next?

"Leonora after your mother, I presume?"

Maria nodded wordlessly, unable to speak as she looked at Walter.

He grinned. "I did not hear that."

"Yes," Maria breathed.

Walter nodded, approval radiating from him, and Maria felt she could melt there, right on the carpet, if she could please him. If she could obey him, bring him pleasure…

"And do you like what I am doing to you?"

Walter had stepped around her, and Maria had known, without him saying a word, that she was not to turn to follow him. She was rewarded as his fingers drifted down her neck and then to the ribbons tying the back of her gown.

"N-No," she managed.

His fingers halted, and Maria felt that warm ache she now recognized as desire starting to build in the pit of her stomach—or just below.

"Please," Maria murmured. "Don't stop."

"You said you did not like what I was doing to you," came the gentle warmth of Walter's mouth on the back of her neck.

Maria shivered. "I just meant…I want more."

It was hard to believe those words had come from her mouth, but Maria could not help it. Here, finally, was someone she could be open with—to whom she could speak the secrets of her heart.

"More?" Walter's fingers resumed their untying and Maria shivered, anticipation building within her. "More what, Maria?"

Scarlet heat burned across her cheeks as Maria's gown slipped, slowly but surely, to pool around her feet.

More what? How could she put into words what she wanted?

How could she speak aloud such scandalous things? Besides, she hardly had the words for some of the things they had already shared, let alone the things she had not yet experienced.

Walter appeared before her with a mischievous grin that made Maria's legs quiver. "I won't take off any more until you answer me, Maria."

Maria almost moaned at the dominant way he spoke to her, that arched eyebrow, that quizzical mouth. What could she do but obey?

"I…I want you to take all my clothes off," Maria breathed.

She saw desire spark in his eyes, his mouth gently falling open as she spoke.

"And then?"

Maria licked her lips, desperately trying to think, and Walter groaned. So, she did have an effect on him, after all. It was rather pleasant to think she was not the only one quivering with desire, desperate to be touched, desperate to be held.

"And…and then," Maria breathed, "I—I want you to touch me."

"Touch you?" repeated Walter, pulling off his own jacket and throwing it to the floor. "Touch you where?"

Wild thoughts scattered through Maria's mind, too dark to speak, too outrageous to utter.

"Do not censure yourself, Maria, or I will not touch you," Walter said, not looking away from her as he pulled off his own waistcoat.

Maria whimpered slightly. Oh, how she wanted to be touched, how she wanted the gap between them to be closed— and if that meant speaking the harlot-like thoughts in her mind, speaking the images into being…

"I want you to touch my breasts," she breathed.

Walter moaned as he pulled off his shirt, revealing a broad chest with hair trailing down to his breeches. "How do you want me to touch them?"

"I…I want you to stroke them. And my…my nipples. I want

you to touch them, tease them, twist them," said Maria, hardly aware of what she was saying, knowing that now the dam of imagination had been broken, it was all going to spill out of her. "I feel alive when you touch my…my breasts."

Walter was breathing slightly heavier than before, Maria noticed, but then, so was she. How was it possible to feel such pooling desire within her, without being touched?

And then she gasped. Walter's fingers were pulling down her underclothes, wrenching them from her, giving her no chance to untie them as they fell to the floor.

She was naked. Absolutely naked, save for her shoes.

Walter's eyes widened as he took her in, and Maria fought the instinct to cover herself. This was it. This was what she wanted, that point of no return.

"And then?" he managed to say, though Maria saw with growing delight that he seemed to be finding speech just as difficult as she was. "Then what do you want?"

"I…" Maria swallowed and tried to think, though it was difficult with such rebellious actions between them. There he stood, half naked. Here she stood, utterly nude. "What do you want?"

Walter appeared rather startled by the question. "Me?"

Maria nodded, taking a step forward, leaving her shoes behind and finding boldness with each step. "What do you want to do to me, Walter?"

She was but a foot from him now.

Walter's gaze dropped down her body, and his voice quavered as he said, "I…well, blast it all, Maria, I would rather like to touch your breasts, too."

"Then do it."

Whether he had been waiting for her permission or just hoped she would make that demand of him, Maria did not know.

What she did know was that as soon as she asked him for it, Walter obeyed.

Maria arched her back into his touch as one of Walter's hands moved to her lower back, pulling her closer, and the other captured her breast, his forefinger and thumb immediately encircling her nipple, twisting it and causing shockwaves of pleasure to rocket through her body.

"Oh," Maria moaned, her eyelashes fluttering in the face of such pleasure. "Oh, Walter…"

She could say no more as her lips were captured by his own, demanding her sweetness, her sensuous tongue, and Maria gave it to him willingly. How could she deny him? Why would she wish to deny such a man anything?

"And now," Walter said, breaking the kiss after such heady moments, Maria could not tell how long they had been standing there, "I am going to kiss you."

Maria blinked blearily up at him. "But you are kissing me."

A wicked smile danced across his lips. "But not there."

Not there? Maria did not understand it—where else was there to—

"Walter!"

It was a good thing she was entirely alone on this corridor, or else Isabella would certainly have heard her pleasured exultation.

Maria placed her hands on Walter's shoulders to steady herself, leaning on them, hardly aware of how she was able to stand up with such ecstasy pouring through her body. She could lean on his shoulders, for he was kneeling before her—his mouth against her secret place, his tongue darting inside her just as it had been teasing her tongue but moments ago.

"Oh, Walter," Maria moaned, unable to think, just to feel.

The way his tongue knew precisely what she wanted—she had thought his fingers expert when he had brought her to pleasure against the tree, but this was something entirely different.

Fast then slow, darting in and out, then gently encircling a part of her throbbing with unrestrained pleasure, Walter's tongue knew precisely what she wanted—and it was not long before Maria could feel the ache building within her, that crest pouring toward her, until she knew she could hold off no longer.

Maria abandoned herself to pleasure. "Oh yes!"

It was fortunate that Walter had lifted his hands to steady her, holding onto her buttocks carefully, for Maria was not entirely sure she would have been able to remain standing without him.

Walter rose to his feet.

"And now," he said in a ragged voice, "it is time to show you real pleasure."

Maria blinked blearily through the haze of sensual delight. "Real pleasure?"

Walter did not reply—not in words. As Maria stood, hardly understanding what he could possibly mean by real pleasure, Walter pulled off his boots and stripped off his breeches.

Maria stared. *Well, she had known in theory what was under those breeches, but it was rather a shock to see it so...so...so much of it.*

"Ready?" breathed Walter.

She nodded, hardly aware what she was agreeing to but knowing if she did not, she would regret it for the rest of her life.

As he sat on the edge of her bed, he offered a hand to her.

"Maria."

"Walter," she whispered as she stepped forward to take his hand. "I...I do not know what to..."

"I will tell you," Walter said with a mischievous grin, still sitting on the bed. "Just do what I say, Maria, and you will experience that pleasure before too long."

Maria could feel herself growing warm again just at the thought of it, and so when he pulled her forward and parted her legs with one hand, she did nothing to stop him.

"Gently," said Walter just under his breath as he pulled her forward an inch, her legs on either side of his own. "Gently..."

"Oh!"

Maria had not expected it. When Walter had gently positioned her over himself and then had taken his hands to her hips and moved her slightly downward, Maria could never have guessed the intensity of the feeling as the very tip of his manhood entered her.

It was unfathomable. His fingers had entered her, his tongue had twisted her into delicious knots, but there was something about this final line they now crossed, Maria slowly edging herself onto Walter's manhood, that was different.

Perhaps it was the way he reacted. Maria marveled as she watched him, his eyes fluttering just as hers had done, and she gloried in the way that, as her hips met his and she had completely sheathed his manhood within her, Walter seemed to ache for more.

"Maria," he croaked.

Maria swallowed, feeling the length of him within her, sparks of pleasure echoing throughout her body. "And is…is this it? We have made love?"

Walter breathed a laugh, and Maria moaned slightly at the shift of him within her. "Not quite, Maria. Now, I am going to help you with the first few, then you can do it on your own."

First few? Maria could not possibly think what the man meant, but as his hands, which had remained on her hips, pulled her up again, just enough to almost allow his manhood out of her, and then pulled her down again onto his manhood, a spark of intense pleasure roared through her.

Walter moaned, and Maria found she had moaned with him. "That was—"

"Again," begged Walter, and it was begging; she could see that.

A flush of power curled around Maria's heart. She could give him pleasure then, just as he had given it to her.

Slowly at first, but growing with confidence with every time, Maria lifted herself and lowered herself. Every bounce seared pleasure through her, sensual decadent pleasure that started from the very center of her but billowed out through her body.

Walter's eyes had half closed, his hands still on her hips, but they did not make her move now. No, he was holding onto her, clinging onto her…

"Oh, Walter," Maria moaned.

She had found the rhythm now, the rhythm Walter had showed her—not just tonight, but before. The pace that brought them closer and closer to that ecstasy, the perfect connection she was so desperate for them to share.

It was building in her, and she could see it building him in, closer, and closer, and as Maria moved against him at a great pace now, panting, Walter did something she had not expected.

Releasing his hands from her hips, they clasped her breasts, forefingers and thumbs around her nipples, and Maria lost all control.

"Yes, yes," she moaned, eyelashes fluttering. "Faster!"

Almost without thought, her own rhythmic bouncing up and down on Walter's manhood increased, and Maria gave herself up to the pace of the pleasure she would now always associate with the man she loved.

"Walter!"

"Maria—oh, yes, yes, yes!"

Something was happening as Maria lost herself to the crest of pleasure—Walter thrust himself up into her, intensifying her pleasure, and Maria clung to him, unable to do anything else.

This was everything. This was what she would have for the rest of her life.

CHAPTER EIGHT

EVERYTHING WAS DIFFERENT—COULD they not see it? Could they not feel it, the difference in the air, the way that everything had completely changed?

Maria could not understand why the entire Fitzroy family could not feel the difference, as she wondered how the whole world could have changed in one night.

Just one night.

Maria shivered slightly as she reached the bottom step of the sweeping Chalcroft staircase and stepped into the hall.

She shivered, not from cold but from the delightful feeling that she had found her place in the world, with Walter. The man she loved, beyond anything. Beyond anyone.

It must be love, this sensation that warmed her even in the coldness of the night. A fire that could not be put out, flames that would never permit themselves to be dampened. An instinct that drew her to him, a knowledge like the geese had that this was where she was supposed to be.

She ached for him, now he was gone, in a way Maria had never experienced before. She craved not just his touch, though she would certainly not reject it if he was to appear.

But it was more than that. There was something about Walter as a man, as a person, that fulfilled her in a way nothing else did. She could feel it within her, a tug to go to the place where she knew she belonged.

Walter's side.

When she had awoken just a few minutes ago, knowing by the chiming of the small mantel clock in her bedchamber that she was significantly late for breakfast, Maria had reached out for the gentleman she had most hoped to speak to.

But Walter was gone.

Maria had sat up, heart falling at the absence of him, before her mind had rightly caught up with her emotions. There was no possibility of him staying with her until breakfast—when the likelihood of him being caught creeping down to the side door was certain.

No, it made sense that Walter had made the wise decision to leave the house before most of the household was awake.

Still. It was disappointing. Maria had so wished to introduce him to her parents, her sisters, so see their delight in her happiness, to see the way he was welcomed by her brothers-in-law.

But that could wait. It would have to.

After hastily dressing, Maria tried to smooth down her skirts and slow down her breathing before she entered the breakfast room. It would certainly not do for her family to guess or even surmise just what she had been doing with Walter not a few hours ago, for their lovemaking had continued on into the night.

"Just do what I say, Maria, and you will experience that pleasure before too long."

Maria swallowed, but the wonderful memories would not disappear. Taking a deep breath, knowing this was as calm as she was likely to be, she stepped forward and entered the breakfast room.

"Good morning," she said quietly.

Not everyone was up yet, it appeared—that, or a few of her family had already been up and breakfasted. Her parents were there, and Isabella, but Olivia, Kitty, and their husbands were absent.

With a lurch to her stomach, Maria realized it was Christmas Eve. *Christmas Eve.* The weeks had gone by so quickly, she had hardly noticed how rapidly they were approaching Christmas Day itself.

Why, today her married sisters had agreed to visit their in-laws—a necessary evil, Kitty had called it; a welcome chance to show familial devotion, Olivia had cut across her.

Maria smiled as she settled herself opposite Isabella and reached for the teapot, steam pouring from its spout. Well, at least that was fewer people to guess what she had done. *What she had enjoyed.*

Maria took a hasty sip of the scalding tea.

She needed to keep her mind on her breakfast and nothing else, Maria told herself sternly. Both of her parents were hidden behind newspapers, and Isabella had brought a book to the breakfast table—against their father's express permission, who did not believe jam should get anywhere near a book, but it did not appear he had noticed.

Maria leaned forward and helped herself to some toast, slathering it with butter. She just had to endure this meal and then she could be out again, seeing Walter. Where would he be? At the cottage, perhaps?

"Oh, it is hopeless!" Leonora threw down the newspaper she had been reading, her face a picture of upset.

Maria stared at her mother. Leonora was known for her outbursts, it was true, but that was just her way.

And this was not anger, either, but hurt. Maria stared at the real pain in her mother's features as she glared at the newspaper, which had apparently so offended her.

Her Papa lowered his own newspaper with a face like thunder. "Not again."

"These people, they will write anything they want, and no one thinks to even ask us, the fools!" spluttered Leonora, jabbing a finger at the offending newspaper. "There should be a law against it!"

Maria glanced at her father, who was shaking his head sadly. "What this time?"

Isabella appeared intrigued, too, and glanced at her mother. "Yes, what is it?"

Most unexpectedly, Leonora looked up at her daughter and flushed. "Oh, Isabella, I did not notice you were...nothing. Nothing at all."

Maria frowned. *Well, one did not have to know her mother well to know she was lying*—but why exclaim loudly about something awful in a newspaper, then immediately pretend that there was nothing in there at all?

It appeared her sister was having the same thought. Red tinging her cheeks, Isabella stuck her chin out. "It is about me, then?"

"I-I do not know where you would get such a wild idea, so wild, so nonsensical," muttered their mother, trying to move the newspaper off the table but Isabella had grabbed one end of it. "Truly, my darling, you do not want to—"

"Where is it?" Isabella said with a sort of forced finality Maria hated to hear.

Isabella was not as gregarious or outgoing as Kitty, nor as elegant nor refined as Isabella. Maria kept to herself so much that Isabella was the sister she knew the least.

But she recognized that look. That was the look Isabella got when she had decided on something and absolutely nothing was going to prevent her from getting her own way.

It was precisely the look their mother had. All four Fitzroy daughters had inherited it.

Isabella wrenched the newspaper out of her mother's hand and flicked through the pages, obviously looking for the gossip column Leonora had been reading.

Their mother turned to their father in desperation. "Tell her not to read it!"

William sighed heavily and put his own newspaper down, and Maria was astonished to see just how resigned he appeared.

"How, my dear? She is a grown woman and can read the newspaper if she wants."

"But…but I don't think…" murmured Leonora, turning back to her daughter.

Maria had not taken her eyes from her sister. Isabella had folded back the newspaper to focus on one particular page, and from the look of her face, she found the content distasteful.

But her curiosity got the better of her. Knowing she should not ask, Maria leaned forward. "What…what does it say?"

Isabella cleared her throat and read aloud from the newspaper in a forced formal voice which grated on Maria's nerves. "We are sorry to reveal that though the London branch of the Fitzroy family seem to be having an excellent time this Christmas season, the same cannot be said of the more senior branch, located at the family's seat in Chalcroft."

"Do not read any more," whispered their mother, her eyes wide. "I beg you."

Maria glanced at her father who seemed in no mood to argue with Isabella—a stance she could hardly disagree with.

Isabella continued, her voice harsh. "While two of the Chalcroft Fitzroy daughters are married and well, this has left a Miss I. Fitzroy quite bereft. Indeed, our correspondent has heard the aforesaid Miss I. is not only lonely this Christmas season but spends most of the year pining over gentlemen she has never met and marriage proposals she has never received."

Maria's jaw dropped. "What?"

"It is an outrage," said their mother stiffly, as though pronouncing judgment to a prisoner in the docks. "An outrage, and if you do not do something, my dear—"

"I cannot forbid speculation, even if it is hurtful to our girls, my dear," said Maria's Papa stiffly. She could see the pain in his eyes, the hurt the article had created not only in Isabella but in their father. "They can print the damned thing if they want to, there is nothing I can do about it."

"Nothing, Papa?" asked Isabella hesitantly. "I mean—where

are they getting it from?"

"Oh, it must be nonsense, just nonsense, wild ideas they are attaching to a random name," cried Leonora vehemently. "I mean, it is not as though the dratted journalist is here, is he? What's his name—Arbor?"

"Arbrow?" said Isabella, glancing back at the article. "No, I suppose…"

She said more. Maria was almost certain that her sister had continued speaking, but what she said, what words she used, what intonation, how she felt…it was all a blur.

Because she could focus on one thing and one thing only. Arbor. Arbrow.

Walter Arborn.

No. It was not possible. Maria would not permit herself to believe it was possible. It was a mistake, a chance, a complete coincidence. There was more than one person in the world with the name of Arborn, after all. At least, she had not precisely met anyone else with the same name, but she had read about them. Read the name many times in…in the newspaper.

A sullen, heavy lead weight fell into her stomach, preventing Maria from eating or drinking. All she could do was sit there at the table and wonder at her own stupidity.

Of course. Of course, it was not real. None of it was true, none of it.

"You are a Fitzroy, of course. One of the beautiful Fitzroys I have heard so much about, and I should have guessed you were Maria. The most beautiful."

"I had…well. Something on my mind that kept me quite preoccupied. Someone."

"Maria, I—there is something I must tell you. I…oh, damn, it is impossible to know where to begin. Maria, I—"

"I love you, too,"

"I…I want you to stroke them. And my…my nipples. I want you to touch them, tease them, twist them. I feel alive when you touch my…my breasts."

Each and every time she had had the opportunity to disbelieve him, every time Walter—Mr. Arborn, for now that was all he could be to her—had given her the chance to doubt him, doubt his word, doubt his character, she had happily swallowed it up. Too infatuated.

For Maria had been desperate to be loved. She could see that now, with all the benefit of hindsight that brought her no joy, only misery.

Her ears were ringing, ringing with all the lies he had told her. Yet of course, there was so little he had told her about himself, wasn't there? All those conversations, all that time they'd spent together…Maria had believed it wonderful, a chance to share her thoughts and ideas, to share them with someone who genuinely was interested in what she had to say.

But it was all a lie. He did not believe her beautiful. He was never pleased to see her—not as a woman, that was, but as a source.

A source. A source for gossip. For the tittle tattle stories of his newspaper.

A huge wave of nausea rose in Maria's stomach.

All these stories in the newspapers, the horrible gossip her family had suffered over the last few days. She had never put the two and two together, but of course, it had only started when Walter had arrived in the neighborhood.

"I—well, I wanted to ask her something as I was so new to the neighborhood, and I thought she might be able to…"

"I…what do you want to know about my mother?"

"I would dearly love to hear it—perhaps I could come to dinner, tonight. Or in a few days, at Christmas. I assume one of these geese is for then?"

Oh, she was so stupid. Maria slumped against the back of her chair, hardly able to believe how foolish she had been. So willing had she been to believe that he was attracted to her, so quick to believe the man she had only just met that he cared for her, even loved her…

He had betrayed her. Walter Arborn had come here looking for stories, hoping for some gossip, and what had she done?

Willingly told him everything.

"My...my mother gives special gifts to the servants. She spends almost all autumn on them—handmade things, you know, made for each servant."

"Isabella? She—she is lonely I think, I am not much company. Oh, Walter!"

And now they were a laughingstock, to the whole world, for who would ever treat the Fitzroy family seriously having read such—such slander! Everything she had said in love and care for her family, Walter had taken and poisoned it, twisted it, made it appear to be so completely different from what it was.

She had trusted him—not only with these stories about her family but with her body. Maria burned with shame to think how easily she had been taken in, when she was nothing but a source for newspaper fodder.

Everything they had shared, which had meant so much to her...the first time any gentleman had ever taken any notice of her...

It had not been special to him. Not like it was for her. Not in the way it made her heart sing, her whole body tingle, her soul think about the future as something exciting and wonderful.

No, Walter just looked at her as a source of gossip. As a lightskirt whom he could tease and make tremble. As a woman he could tup, then toss aside.

Maria swallowed, trying to force down these awful thoughts, but she could not help it, painful as they were. She needed to know just how much she had been betrayed.

How she had, in turn, betrayed her family.

She looked up, blinking. Her father and mother were still arguing about the best way to go about contradicting the gossip— her father favored his solicitor, though admitted there was little the man could probably do—while her mother appeared to be suggesting assault.

Her sister, Isabella, was sitting quietly on the other side of the table. All the harshness and bitterness had seeped from her. She looked small, defeated, exhausted.

Maria's heart ached for her, but selfishly it mostly ached for herself.

Just a few hours ago, she had believed she had shared one of the most important moments of her life with a man who truly mattered to her, with whom she shared mutual affection.

Nothing else would have convinced her to share that innermost part of herself. What had so recently been exquisite joy was now desperate agony.

He had not loved her, nor cared for her.

Perhaps he had not even enjoyed it.

"And now, it is time to show you real pleasure."

"Real pleasure?"

Maria swallowed. Remembering the words of love he had spoken to her was not going to heal her heart any sooner. She would have to put all those thoughts aside; Walter had surely been lying. She could not trust a single word that came from his mouth.

Just when she had been so certain she had found the person she wished to be with for the rest of her days...she had instead been deceived.

Shame poured through her—shame Maria knew she deserved. She had been tricked, yes, but she had been a willing participant in the farce, so quick to believe a man like that could care for her, could love her.

He had always been so interested in her family, had he not? In her, too, yes, later—but at first, what were all his questions about?

Her mother. Her family.

Maria placed her head in her hands as the argument raged around the breakfast table. Well, she would not be the first woman taken in by a liar. She would just have to hope Walter Arborn would return to London soon, and she could be left here in Chalcroft to grow old on the memories, though tainted, that they had shared.

The door to the hall opened, and a footman cleared his throat. "Mr. Walter Arborn, sir."

CHAPTER NINE

MARIA TRULY BELIEVED her heart had stopped. She could not feel it beating. She could not feel anything. Numbness had spread through her body like ice, like a cooling flood that dampened all passion she had once felt.

"Mr. Walter Arborn, sir."

There he was. Standing behind the footman, smiling. *Smiling.* As though he did not care about her at all. As though he thought it was funny, this decision he had taken to betray them all.

As though he should be congratulated.

Nausea rose in Maria's stomach, but there was nothing she could do, nothing she could say. It was as though she had been frozen, unable to speak or move, to warn her family that the man who had betrayed them so utterly was now in the room with them.

Except…

Except he was not the only one who had betrayed them, was he? The painful truth of the matter was, and Maria was only now starting to realize it, she had betrayed them, too.

"Isabella? She—she is lonely I think, I am not much company. Oh, Walter!"

Maria swallowed. She had not intended to betray them. Had not realized the questions she had been asked were so leading, had not known her words would be twisted and defiled, put in a newspaper for the world to laugh at them…

But that did not matter. The point was, Maria realized with a sinking feeling, it had happened.

And now she would have to undo all the pain she had wrought, all the more difficult while looking into the smiling, handsome face of Walter Arborn—the man she had been convinced had loved her.

Loved her. Maria quivered slightly with fury as she considered the words.

Walter did not understand the meaning of love.

"Mr. Arborn?" her Papa said mildly, his back to the door, and therefore unable to see Walter. "Who is—"

Maria stood up. "Mr. Arborn and I have business to discuss."

Her father blinked at her in mild confusion, while the rest of the table turned to stare.

Isabella swallowed. "The drawing room is available—Maria, should you need a chaperone, I—"

"I am quite capable of speaking to a gentleman for ten minutes without the need of a chaperone, thank you," said Maria, hating every word she spoke. The lies she uttered.

She certainly had not been when it came to Mr. Walter Arborn.

Oh, she had been a fool. So easily lulled into a false sense of security, so easily able to believe he had come for her, wished to see her, wished to kiss her…

Walter's smile had become a smirk, and Maria glared at him as she moved around the table toward the door. His smile did not falter. The dratted man thought she was pleased to see him but had to keep up a pretense before her family.

Well, he would soon discover just how wrong he was.

The footman opened the drawing room door, but Maria strode past him to the front door, opening it and indicating that Walter should go through.

"Thank you, that will be all," she said formally to the servant as he waited awkwardly.

The man bobbed his head and disappeared. Walter stepped outside, that dratted smile still on his face, and Maria followed him, heart now beating so fast it was almost a whir.

She had to do this. She had to have this conversation, had to because she knew she would not be able to live with herself if she did not. The drawing room was too likely to have one of her sisters on the other side of a door, listening.

Outside would be better—in the farm, where there was copious amounts of noise. No one would think to look for them there.

"The goose pen," she said shortly.

Maria did not look at him as she spoke. She could not bear to, the man to whom she had given her heart. Well, she would have to claim it back now she thought as her feet crunched on the snow, pacing towards the goose pen as though her life depended on it.

Maria had made a mistake, yes, but it had been innocently made. She now had to tell him that she knew now what he had done, what he was.

And that she wanted nothing more to do with him.

Reaching the goose pen, absolutely swarming with birds, Maria leaned against it and looked at Walter, so quickly at ease in the outdoors of Chalcroft. He leaned against the fence, lolling rather resplendently, and Maria's heart broke.

He was so handsome. So charming. He made her feel—even before he had touched her, he had made her feel...special. *Desired.*

But it had all been a lie.

Walter grinned, but his smile slowly faded as he took in her expression. "Maria?"

Maria swallowed. If only she'd had time, after realizing just what a cad and liar the man was, to think about what she must say to him. There could not have been five minutes between her realization and the man himself appearing.

She had no clever words prepared, no speech, no cutting

remarks that would show Walter she had found him out.

Staying calm was difficult. Her stomach lurched painfully, threatening to overwhelm her. But she had to do this. She had to say something.

"You…you were using me."

The words crept out of her mouth before she could stop them. Maria looked at Walter directly, the wintery sunshine seeping down on them but giving no warmth.

Walter shook his head slowly. "No—no, Maria, I had to leave early this morning, otherwise there would be a chance I could be discovered. You do see that, don't you?"

He thought she was talking about their lovemaking. Maria almost laughed bitterly at the mistake. It was no longer just about her; perhaps, in a way, it had never been about her.

"No," she said, trying to keep her voice level, but struggling. "I do not mean that."

Walter frowned as he examined her, as though he would understand what she meant merely by looking at her. Maria welcomed his gaze for a moment, knowing that in a few minutes he would never look at her like that again.

He would never *look* at her again. She would certainly never permit him to enter Chalcroft.

"Well, if he comes to the front door again, you are not to let him in, you understand?"

Maria's heart ached. Oh, if only she had listened to him; if only she had heeded her father's words. Not just the words, but what he was trying to say.

If she had taken him seriously, she would never have fallen in love with a man who could so easily betray her. Betray all of them.

Maria swallowed and took a deep breath. "You…you…"

But the words were not in her.

Distress growing in her heart and not knowing what to do, Maria turned away from Walter, unable to look at him, and instead looked at the geese. They were happily squawking away, minding their own business.

Her mind wandered, taking her back to the last conversation that she and Walter had had in this very place.

"You know the old fairytale, the goose that laid the golden eggs."

And it came to her. Maria finally understood, though it was painful to accept.

"I am the golden egg."

"I beg your pardon?" said Walter, clearly bewildered. "You are—I must have misheard you."

But Maria was growing in courage, now she understood. Oh, it was so simple. He needed stories, and here she was, a ready-made goose laying golden eggs. Whenever he needed something, she gave it to him. Even if she did not know it.

"Golden egg," Maria repeated, finally looking at him and taking in his bewilderment. *Well, he would not be confused for much longer.* "Every time you needed a story to sell about my family, a little piece of gossip you could twist and poison, you came to me. And I gave it to you, did I not, Walter Arborn?"

All the color drained from Walter's face. Maria watched it with a strange sort of cold satisfaction. *She had been right, then.* There was a strange comfort in knowing she was right.

"Maria," said Walter in a low voice, "it is not what you—"

"It is exactly what I think," said Maria in a hiss. "You—you are a journalist!"

"You say that as though it is a crime," Walter said coldly.

Maria laughed bitterly, unable to help herself. "Yes, I suppose I do—but then who would blame me, after seeing the ridiculous stories you have been writing about my family!"

"I did not write them," Walter said quickly. "All I did was—"

"I do not care if *you* wrote them or someone else did or your fairy godmother did!" Maria said heatedly. *How dare he speak to her like that, as though—as though she were a child! As if the specifics mattered!* "The point is you gave them details about me, my family, people that I love, and you made my loving words sound awful!"

Walter's face was still pale, and he appeared agitated, but Maria would not permit herself to feel sorry for him. All he had done was lie, hide who he was, lie to get what he wanted.

He deserved no pity from her.

"It was not like that, I never intended for your words to be twisted and changed and—I never intended this to happen!"

Maria stared. Walter had almost shouted those words, desperate to convince her of his innocence, though he surely could not believe she would be so easily taken in.

"Walter, you told someone what I told you, and you saw what was printed," Maria said slowly and coldly. "You knew they were not going to report the truth, though heaven knows why you were interested in my family to begin with!"

Walter frowned slightly at her. "You...you really thought it was about your family?"

His surprise wrong footed her. Maria opened her mouth but closed it again, unsure what to say. He spoke as though it was obvious, as though there was something in her family that was of note in the first place.

"N-No," she found herself saying, despite herself.

Walter raised an eyebrow. "Well, that would explain why I could not get anything out of you."

Maria blinked. It did not make sense. But then she realized just how quickly he had distracted her, and his true intent had slipped out, damned by his own tongue.

Well, that would explain why I could not get anything out of you.

She must not lose sight of the anger she felt, the rage that poured through her. Maria felt it rise within her once more and fanned the flames, knowing that only by remaining angry at Walter could she say what she needed to say.

"You treated me like the goose who laid the golden eggs," Maria said quietly, vengefully, her eyes focused on him. "Your only interest in me were the stories I could feed you—you did not care for me!"

"That is not true," said Walter. "Perhaps at first, but—"

"And whenever you needed another story," Maria interrupted, knowing she had to get it all out before her voice choked with emotion, "you came back to get another one! No wonder you…you bedded me. Getting closer to the source!"

"It was not like that!" Walter looked truly upset by her words, but Maria knew better than to trust a man who could lie to her so easily. "I admit, it started off as—well, as useful to know you, but Maria, that changed so quickly! From the very first moment I kissed you—"

"You should never have done that," said Maria, looking away, unable to look at him as she thought of how easily she had been won.

Stepping away from him around the pen, she wondered whether she should just return to the house. This was too painful, too shameful. Had she not brought enough shame on the family already?

A hand grasped at hers, and she turned to see Walter had stepped forward.

"Let," said Maria darkly, hatred dripping off each syllable, "go of me."

Walter dropped her hand, hurt across his face. "Maria, I love—"

"Do not say it, I beg you, for I have no wish to hear your lies any longer," said Maria helplessly. "Please, Walter, just go."

"I am not lying—"

"Really?" Maria raised an eyebrow, and Walter flinched at her tone. "You treated me like a goose laying golden eggs, Walter, and—"

"I would give up six geese a laying golden eggs!" Walter urged her, looking desperately into her eyes. "Don't you understand me, Maria, I am trying to tell you that I love you!"

Maria's heart contracted slightly, but she refused to allow herself to be so easily won over. Oh, how she would have liked to hear that only yesterday—and now she came to think about it, when they had been outside the side door, it was she who had confessed and declared her love for Walter.

But had he done the same?

She tried to think, tried to remember past the sweet ecstasy they had shared that night.

No. Walter had never said anything about his affections. It was only now, now he was losing his source, that he was so passionate.

Maria hardened her heart and forced herself to look at him. "I don't believe you."

"I tried to tell you all about this yesterday!" Walter sounded desperate, as though his life depended on her believing him. "Maria, do you not remember? I tried to tell you how this had started, how it had changed for me, changed irrevocably, and you did not let me speak!"

She wished to argue with him, to declare he was a liar—lying then and lying now.

But a memory seeped into her mind…

"Maria, I—there is something I must tell you. I…oh, damn, it is impossible to know where to begin. Maria, I—"

Maria swallowed. How close she had been to the truth, yet she had been so sure Walter was about to declare his love for her. So certain she had presumed to declare her own feelings first.

Oh, if only she had permitted him to talk. If she had heard the truth then, she would never have invited the sneaking man into her home, her bedchamber, her very body.

She would not have lost her innocence to a man who simply could not be trusted.

"Well, I wish you had made more of an effort to be honest with me," she said coldly.

"Argh!" Walter exclaimed angrily, twisting away from her for a moment as though to compose himself, then turning back with a beseeching look on his face that before today, would have had a great impact on her heart. "Maria, do you not think it possible for a man to make a mistake? To—to fall into bad habits, bad practices, bad company, then to realize too late what he has become?"

Maria stared. It was a wonderful sort of image—the idea that Walter had merely been led astray, that he was not a bad man in himself, but had instead been tempted away from goodness.

But a good man would not have stroked her into submission, into sensuous pleasure against a tree trunk in the woods where anyone could have come across them…

"I do believe it is possible for a man to make a mistake," Maria said quietly, and she watched Walter's face relax with relief until she continued. "One mistake. You, Walter, have made several."

"Maria—"

"I am aware of three stories, at least three, about my family which have been printed most heinously and with mistruths," said Maria, forcing herself to continue. Tears were threatening to fall, and she would not permit herself to cry, not before Walter Arborn. "Those are just the ones I know about. You did not make one mistake. You made several, knowing you were betraying me—yes, betraying!"

Walter's face had contorted with pain at the word. "You cannot think so ill of me."

"No?" Maria shook her head slowly. "I think worse."

"I never intended those snippets to go to print!"

"You used me." Maria made sure she emphasized each of her words, watching Walter flinch at each one. It was important he knew, understood. That he saw the pain in her own face. "You think I could trust you again after knowing what you have done? How little regard and respect you gave me? Walter, you may think yourself in love, and I am sure that is a fine and pretty thing, but really? Really, you just desire power, knowledge, the opportunity to better yourself."

Walter was shaking his head, eyes sparkling with unshed tears. "No—no, Maria, I love you—perhaps not as I ought to have done, but—"

"It does not matter if you love me," said Maria softly. Her

heart was breaking and soon it would be too much, but she had to continue. "It does not matter. I...I can never see you the same way. You are not the man I thought you were, so you are not the man I cared for. Please leave Chalcroft, Mr. Arborn, you are not wanted here."

Turning away from Walter and the goose pen, Maria stormed away, feet taking her hastily back toward Chalcroft. As tears ran down her face and her throat choked with unuttered sobs, she knew she would never see him again. Never be touched like that again.

Never love again.

CHAPTER TEN

"CHRISTMAS DAY IS a day to be joyful!" The vicar beamed round at his congregation, dressed in his finery and with arms wide open. "A day to be with those we love, a day to celebrate all that is good and great about this world…"

Maria tried to concentrate. She really did. She knew it would be most scandalous if she did not, as the entire Fitzroy family was seated in their pew at the front of the church. The entire congregation could undoubtedly see that she was not concentrating, but what could she do?

The argument from yesterday was ringing in her mind, making it impossible to pay attention to the sermon the Reverend was now attempting to give.

"—and as we celebrate this day—"

"Well, I wish you had made more of an effort to be honest with me."

"Such a glorious day for being with those we care for. A time for family, a time to embrace those we care for…"

"Maria, do you not think it possible for a man to make a mistake? To—to fall into bad habits, bad practices, bad company, then to realize too late what he has become?"

"—thinking on this day as a time for reconciliation, of peace…"

"I am aware of three stories, at least three, about my family which have been printed most heinously and with mistruths. Those are just the

ones I know about. You did not make one mistake. You made several, knowing you were betraying me—yes, betraying!"

Maria swallowed back the tears that were threatening to form at the corners of her eyes, as she attempted not to think about the argument she had endured with Walter—with Mr. Arborn just the day before.

Had it not been enough that she had suffered the ignominy of falling in love with a man who had absolutely no true affection for her?

Was it not hard enough that her time with him had been based on lies, that she could not trust a single thing that he said?

"You cannot think so ill of me."

"No. I think worse."

No, it was far worse. Maria had given herself, had given everything. Everything she had expected to share with her true love, the gentleman who would be with her for the rest of her life…

And now she had squandered it.

"And now, it is time to show you real pleasure."

"Real pleasure?"

A small tear threatened to fall, and she brushed it away angrily. She would not permit herself to think any longer of him. She could not allow herself to do that.

Besides, it was most unfair. She was the one who had been betrayed, lied to, tricked—and Walter had the gall to act as though he was equally hurt when she discovered his falsehoods!

Maria cleared her throat and tried desperately to focus on the Christmas Day sermon. It could not go on much longer, could it? The man had been talking for nigh on an hour. At least, that was what it felt like.

She had attempted to avoid coming to church this morning at all, but her mother had been having none of it.

"It is Christmas Day!" Leonora had spluttered, adjusting her bonnet carefully in the looking glass in the hall. "Christmas Day, Maria! Why on earth would you want to stay at home and miss the service?"

Her sisters had looked at Maria curiously, Kitty attempting to chase after a toddler who had made a run for it across the hall to the stairs, giggling as he went.

And Maria had felt the overwhelming need to hide what she had done, forever, from them all. How could they understand? How could they ever forgive her for abandoning all her principles and permitting Walter to…to…

The thought of what she had allowed Walter to do, what they had done to each other, shared together, had made Maria's cheeks flush.

Thankfully, however, her family seemed entirely accustomed to Maria's flushes.

"Whatever it is, you can tell us about it after church," her father had said firmly. "Best bonnet on, please."

Maria sighed in the pew, desperately hoping the Reverend would be finished soon. *Surely there was simply not that much more to say about Christmas…was there?*

"And if we go back to the book of Genesis," said the Reverend with a broad smile, "we will see…"

Maria sighed but sat up a little straighter after being elbowed by Olivia.

"Be quiet," her sister hissed. "What has got into you, anyway?"

There was no possible way of explaining to the eldest Fitzroy daughter—now Lady Kingsley, of course—just what had got into her.

A wry smile crept across Maria's face. Not if she wasn't going to tell anyone precisely what Walter and she had shared together.

"Nothing," she whispered.

Olivia raised an eyebrow, as if to show without words she was entirely unimpressed by Maria's words and would certainly be asking more about it later, but said nothing.

That was one of the few benefits of being stuck here in church, she supposed. At least she did not have to explain herself. And from what she could see, Walter had not attended.

As if he would have been able to face her, Maria thought with a lump in her throat. Why, he had hardly managed to explain himself yesterday, had he? Completely unable to justify the way he had behaved.

It was outrageous.

"—in peace, to love and serve the Lord."

Maria blinked. The reverend was bowing his head to his congregation and murmured replies of good cheer and best wishes echoed around her.

Was that it? Was it finally over?

"An excellent service, I thought," said William brightly. "Truly excellent—and never have I before heard those two Bible passages brought together. What did you think, Maria?"

Maria blinked at her father. "I beg your pardon?"

"Ignore her," said Olivia breezily. "Maria has a headache."

Maria stared at her older sister. Why on earth had she lied? It was most unlike Olivia to volunteer information like that, especially when it was entirely false.

"A headache!" Leonora bemoaned. "Oh, Maria, why did you not say?"

Maria caught Olivia's eye and saw she was going to have to repay that favor, perhaps in the not-too-distant future. Her nephews would have a nursemaid this afternoon, it seemed.

"I did not wish to worry you, Mama," said Maria weakly.

William shook his head. "I do wish you had told us, Maria. I certainly would not have insisted that you accompany us to church. Come, let us go home."

Relief soared through Maria's heart. *Yes, home.* Where she could be alone. Where she could avoid all the consequences of her rash actions. Where she could hide away from any opportunity of seeing Walter.

Bright wintery sunlight hit her eyes as she stepped out of the church, and for a moment, she could not see a thing. When her vision slowly came back into view, it was with a jolt to her stomach that she saw a gentleman waiting outside for her.

Walter.

"Mr. Arborn," said Maria's father stiffly. "Good day."

His dismissive tone, however, did not seem to have any effect on the young man, who stepped forward. "Maria—"

"I do not want to talk to you," said Maria quickly, hating how she could not bear for her family to see her like this. Broken. Betrayed. "Go away."

"No," said Walter firmly. "I just need to tell you—"

"We'll see you at the house," said Olivia firmly, taking her mother's arm. "Papa?"

Maria stared at her sister. *What on earth did she think she was doing?* Couldn't Olivia see that there was absolutely no chance that she wanted to speak with Walter? The man was a disgrace, a wretch, a—

"Do not be too long," Olivia shot back over her shoulder as she shepherded the rest of the Fitzroys away. "Luncheon is in an hour."

"But..."

Maria knew what she wanted to say. At least, she had a vague idea. She could not permit her family to just disappear. She needed them beside her, supporting her, protecting her.

But at the same time, she did not wish them to see just how entirely destroyed she was by Walter's betrayal of her. Of them all. She was not, after all, the only Fitzroy who had suffered because of his lies.

The rest of the congregation were thinning now, disappearing off to their homes, their Christmas lunches, a few presents for the children and singing around the pianoforte. Soon, far too soon, Maria was conscious it was just the two of them.

"Maria," said Walter, taking a step toward her.

"I said I do not want to speak with you," said Maria stiffly, walking along the path away from the church, trying desperately not to meet Walter's eyes. "Can I make myself more plain?"

He was being impossible; impossibly handsome, impossibly irritating, Maria could barely think she was so infuriated.

How dare he come here—how dare he approach her? Outside church, with her family, too!

He was absolutely the most irritating—

"Walter!" Maria cried at the sudden shock of having her hands grabbed by the gentleman who did not understand she wished to be left quite alone. "Walter, what are you—"

"You have to listen to me," said Walter firmly, pulling her up the path to the cottage he had rented from the vicar. "Whether you want to or not—hear my side of the story, then you can make your decision."

Maria would have said something impressive and cutting—if, of course, she could think. Her hands were scalding hot from his touch, even through her gloves, and she glanced back quickly to see if anyone had spotted her being dragged off into woodland by a gentleman.

But there was no one there. They were alone.

"Look," Walter said firmly, stopping and looking deep into her eyes.

Maria looked away. She had trusted those eyes, believed them when he had spoken words of affection, when he had teased her into giving away stories of her family, stories she had not believed could be harmful, but of course were.

Eyes she had looked into as they found pleasure together…

Maria swallowed and forced herself to harden her heart. This was not a man she could trust. This was not a man who she would allow back into her heart.

"You have to believe me," said Walter, his breath short. "I had no idea what they were going to write about you, about your family."

Maria laughed bitterly, trying to make it abundantly clear she believed him not a jot. *The cheek of it!* Here they stood, outside the cottage he was renting from the reverend—from a man of the cloth!—and he had the audacity to lie again!

"Spare me your excuses, they are both pathetic and immaterial," said Maria, finding a strength within she did not know she had.

Walter wilted at her words. "You...you do not what to know the full story?"

"You think anything can possess me to take a word of yours seriously?" Maria was incredulous; the man was a fool indeed. "You have done naught but lie to me from the moment I first met—"

"That is not true," said Walter hastily, color growing in his cheeks. "Everything I have said to you about how I feel—"

"And the worst of it all was that I wanted to believe you!" Maria could hardly believe it of herself. So easily tricked, so easily misled... "I wanted to believe you cared for me, that it was for me and me alone that you continued coming to Chalcroft—but it wasn't, was it?"

Walter opened his mouth, his face fierce as though he would oppose her immediately...then his face fell, and he closed his mouth.

His lack of defense was almost as bad as a poor one. Maria's stomach lurched painfully, her heart skipping a beat. A part of her, and she would not admit just how large, had rather hoped he did have a perfectly good argument, a defense, a way to explain away what he had done.

That his betrayal was not in fact, a betrayal.

But he had nothing to say. Nothing at all.

"So, you were sent here," Maria said, far more calmly than she felt, "to spy on us. To dig some—what is it Papa said? Some dirt on us, on my family. Why?"

Walter shrugged, looking far more helpless yet with a flicker of anger in his tones. "Why? You think they tell me anything— you think I have any control what goes on in that paper? Maria, I am a dogsbody, someone they have in the office in London to fetch and carry. Never allowed to do much, always forbidden from opportunities. I saw my chance, my opportunity to finally prove myself—"

"And all it took was traitorous lies," Maria finished off harshly.

Far more harshly than she felt. It was most unfair that the man was so handsome, so believable as he spoke. But was it her fault? Had she been the one to cast him down, to prevent him from rising in his occupation? Why did it have to be her family to suffer the consequences?

"I admit," said Walter heavily, "at first, our interactions, our conversations…it was all about the stories."

Maria took an unsteady step backward. Even now, when she believed there was nothing else awful to hear, Walter was able to surprise her. Able to demonstrate how callous he truly was.

"Until that kiss."

Her gaze jerked up. "Kiss?"

Their first kiss. A moment of sweet perfection. One she could never get back now of course, but Maria had not cared. She had wanted Walter. The softness, the sweetness, and yet the sensual way he had possessed her. Claimed her. Devoured her.

It had tinged her dreams and made some of her daydreams far too indecent to be thought of again.

And it had affected him, too? She was not the only one to feel it?

"From that very moment, I knew you were different," said Walter quietly, a nervous smile tweaking his lips. "Knew I had got myself into far more trouble than I had ever bargained for. Knew I was in danger of…"

Danger of what? Maria was too embarrassed to ask, but there was a hint of it around his eyes.

If only she could trust him. *If only Walter had proven himself to be a man of honor…*

"I tried to convince myself my role was perfect because it brought me closer to you," Walter said with a laugh. "Pathetic, I know. I was just trying to trick myself into believing there was no harm brought to you if I saw you again. And again…"

Maria could not help a smile creeping across her face. "I also tried to convince myself no harm could come if I spent time with you."

Walter met her eyes, and for a moment, a flashing moment, Maria could forget all the revelations which had brought her such pain. Forget he had betrayed her, lied to her, had made a mockery of her sister…

Isabella's face appeared in Maria's mind, sharp and painful. The agony in her sister's expression when she thought about how Society would now be laughing at her, mocking her…

"They can print the damned thing if they want to, there is nothing I can do about it."

"Nothing, Papa? I mean—where are they getting it from?"

Maria swallowed and turned away. "Yet you betrayed me, betrayed my family."

"I tell you again, I never dreamed they would write such things," said Walter, moving to catch her eye—unsuccessfully. "I thought it a column about gentry families, about eligible young ladies, about where their parents came from and so I—"

"Saw me as the golden egg that could get you up the ladder," said Maria dully. "A silly goose. A goose you have now killed, by the way. I will never tell you any other stories. You have lost your golden opportunity."

Well, this was why her Mama had always said it was difficult to marry a man in trade. She had considered Walter a gentleman, a true gentleman, but he was a grasping, eager—

"I regret it now. I regret it all."

Maria nodded; she could not help herself. "Because you have lost your source."

"Because I have lost my soulmate!"

Suddenly her hands were taken again, and Maria gasped as Walter pulled her close, his chest pressed up against hers.

"Maria, you have to believe me—each moment with you was perfection, and I quickly realized I could do nothing but be with you," said Walter earnestly. "If you cannot forgive me…well, I will settle for bachelorhood for the rest of my days. But if you can find it in your heart to forgive me…"

It was all too much, too overwhelming—and Maria knew she could not stand it.

Because she cared about him too much. As she looked up into Walter's eyes, she saw the hope, the desperation. The need to have her, and it was intoxicating. Had she ever been desired like this before? Had she ever been truly wanted, by anyone?

"I…" Walter swallowed, and Maria found herself willing him to speak. "I love you, Maria. Truly. More than I think anyone has loved anyone else."

Maria stared up at him. *What did he want from her? What was she supposed to say?*

"And I suppose the only thing left to do," Walter said quietly, "is to prove it."

Slowly, very slowly, he leaned down, further and further, still holding onto Maria's hands and not looking away from her widening eyes.

"Walter, what are you—"

"Maria Fitzroy," said Walter from a kneeling position.

Maria stared. This was impossible—this was surely not happening! It was not the sort of thing that happened to people like her—this happened to Olivia and Kitty and their cousins.

Not her. *No one wished to marry her…surely not…*

"I love you. I want to marry you—and I want to earn back your trust. If that means an engagement of months—years, even!—then I am willing," said Walter earnestly. His eyes shone brightly, unshed tears appearing in the corners. "Maria, I have made a mistake and it was a terrible one, but I must hope your affection for me can overcome it. I am truly remorseful, and more in love with you than ever. Please. Please, be my wife."

For a heartstopping moment, Maria stood there, unsure what to do, hardly aware of how to breathe.

So, this was it. She had received her first and likely only proposal—from a man whom she loved desperately, yet who had been given her plenty of reasons not to trust him.

The way he kissed…the places of her he kissed…

Was that enough? Was love, deep love and affection, lust and desire, pleasure and play, enough to overcome all her doubts?

"Maria?"

Maria laughed breathlessly, and shrugged her shoulders as she said, "I…I do not know if I can marry a journalist!"

Walter's eyes widened. "Then—then you accept?"

"I did not say that," said Maria hurriedly as Walter rose to his feet. "I said I did not know if I could marry a journalist."

"You know, I am not sure whether I could either," said Walter matter-of-factly.

Maria stared at this impossible man. "I beg your pardon?"

"Well, I suppose I could always fall back on my trade, though I did vow I never would," said Walter with a nervous laugh. "You'll be rather surprised, I think, to discover that I actually trained as a…well. A solicitor."

Maria's mouth fell open as birdsong started in the trees behind her. "A lawyer?"

"You say that like a curse," said Walter with a nervous smile. "Yes, a lawyer."

Well, now she had heard everything. *How on earth was she supposed to know what to do with a man like this—a man who seemed to delight in nothing more than confusing her!*

"You are a lawyer," she repeated.

He shrugged. "I grew bored of it, to tell you the truth…working in the papers seemed far more exciting. But yes, I am a lawyer, and with a rather good practice that keeps ticking over, thanks to my assistant."

Maria could not take it in. A gentleman with a trade. A respected, educated gentleman who did not depend on the newspapers for a living—who would never fall into that mistake again.

"I have so much to tell you about myself," Walter spoke softly, rising to his feet and pulling Maria into his arms. "And we will have the rest of our lives for me to do that if…if you will…"

Perhaps it was the revelation that he was not a dyed-in-the-wool journalist. Perhaps it was the way he looked at her. Perhaps it was neither of those things, but something else entirely. Maria was not sure.

Whatever the reason, she knew deep within herself, that the adventure she would take with Walter, no matter where he took her, would be far more enjoyable than anything else she could imagine.

"I will," Maria breathed.

It would have been impossible for her to say anything else, even if she had wanted to. Walter pulled her forward, his lips crushing hers, and Maria almost cried out for joy as they connected once more as lovers. As they always should have done.

She clung to him, desperate to take in as much of him as she could, and when they finally broke away, she could tell there was but one thing on his mind.

"Your cottage is right there," Maria whispered, feeling a thrill rush through her at the scandalous suggestion.

Walter glanced over his shoulder and grinned. "So it is."

Maria shrieked with laughter as he pulled her toward it, her heart soaring. *So, this was it.* She would marry Walter, leave behind the Fitzroy name, and become a Arborn.

This was what her entire life had been leading up to and she could not believe she was so happy. Indeed, she—

"Walter!" Maria exclaimed as he pushed her toward the bay window of the cottage and propped her up against the window-sill. "What do you think you're doing?"

A wicked grin appeared on his face. "Precisely what you think I am doing."

One hand fumbled with the buttons on his breeches while the other started pushing her skirts to her knees.

"Walter Arborn!" Maria hissed, trying to pull down her skirts against his supple fingers. "There is a path right there, anyone could come walk by and see!"

"I know," said Walter in a low voice, kissing Maria's neck and causing shivers of pleasure to ripple through her. "Exciting, isn't it?"

Maria could not help it. She moaned, the intensity of his kissing down her neck and toward her collarbone too much. What a man he was, what dexterity of tongue and fingers. She would spend the rest of her life being pleasured like this and pleasuring in return. It was almost too much…

"Ready?"

Maria opened her eyes and saw Walter's breeches around his ankles and knew she should not. Knew they should not.

"Geese never fly alone."

"No, they fly together. One leading at the front, all the others following them…"

But she knew she could just as easily have told a goose to stop flying, to stop following the one at the front. It was impossible. She knew where this route went, and her whole body was tingling in anticipation.

"Take me," she whispered.

Walter did not need any further invitation. Thrusting forward as he pushed Maria's skirts back and pulled her buttocks forward, he entered her, and Maria gasped at the intensity of it all.

Here she was, propped up against a windowsill, being possessed and pounded by him—and she would not have wished to be anywhere else.

"Oh, Walter," she whimpered as she clutched his buttocks, unable to do anything but sit there and take the pleasure.

"Damn, Maria, you feel so good," moaned Walter, his rhythm increasing, sparking pleasure across Maria's body. "God, I missed you—"

"I missed you so much," Maria cried, clutching him as the waves of pleasure threatened to soar over her more quickly than she could have predicted. "I want more, more, more, yes!"

Allowing her head to fall back, unable to lift it as she was overcome by ecstasy, Maria's body shivered as searing hot pleasure washed over her, rocking her whole body.

"Maria!"

Walter's thrusts became jerky, irregular, as he lost himself to his own crest, and Maria welcomed him into her arms as he collapsed into her.

Heart frantically beating, her body tingling with the forbidden erotic moment they had just shared, the scandalous thought that anyone could have come across them at any moment…

Maria clutched Walter to her and luxuriated in the sensation of closeness.

"You silly goose," he murmured as he kissed her neck. "You do know I will always love you, don't you?"

"You had better," said Maria with a wry smile as she allowed herself to be loved. "Or no golden eggs for you."

About Emily E K Murdoch

If you love falling in love, then you've come to the right place.

I am a historian and writer and have a varied career to date: from examining medieval manuscripts to designing museum exhibitions, to working as a researcher for the BBC to working for the National Trust.

My books range from England 1050 to Texas 1848, and I can't wait for you to fall in love with my heroes and heroines!

Follow me on twitter and instagram @emilyekmurdoch, find me on facebook at facebook.com/theemilyekmurdoch, and read my blog at www.emilyekmurdoch.com.